"That's why you applied to the official case, Lyndsey.

"I knew that sometime, someplace, I'd want nothing more than to make love to you."

"After what happened last time?"

R.J.'s thumbs moved in slow, hypnotic circles on her cheeks, and when he spoke, the heat of his breath brushed her face. "I said, 'make love,' Lyndsey, not just have sex. I want to show you the difference."

Every part of her crystallized into a need for this man. But she also felt fear. "I'm afraid I'll disappoint you."

"You? Never," he said in a low voice.

A shiver rippled through her when she thought of how little she'd had to give in the past. "But, I—"

His voice was low and hoarse. "Do you want me?"

The expression in his eyes made her tremble. "Yes," she breathed. "I want you."

Dear Reader,

The holiday season is in full swing, and most of us are busy running around buying, wrapping—and hiding—gifts for our families and friends. But it's important not to forget ourselves during this hectic time, and Silhouette Intimate Moments is here with four terrific romances for you to enjoy when you steal a few moments on your own.

First up is Emilie Richards with *Twilight Shadows,* a tie-in to her last book for the line, *Desert Shadows.* Things are never what they seem in the movies anyway, but in this case we're talking about some *real* desperate characters and bad actors. Pick up the book and you'll see what I mean!

After a long—too long!—absence, favorite author Kathleen Eagle returns to Intimate Moments with *Bad Moon Rising.* Kathleen is deservedly celebrated for her portrayals of Native American characters, and this book once again demonstrates why. And for those of you who remember her long-ago Silhouette Christmas story, "The Twelfth Moon," there's an extra treat in store. I guess this book is in the way of being a Christmas present, too!

Mary Anne Wilson's *Nowhere To Run* and Marilyn Cunningham's *Long White Cloud* round out the month. And next year (!) look for more of your favorite authors—Heather Graham Pozzessere, Kathleen Korbel, Dallas Schulze and Kathleen Creighton, to name only a few—coming to you in Silhouette Intimate Moments.

Happy Holiday Reading!

Leslie Wainger
Senior Editor and Editorial Coordinator

MARY ANNE WILSON

Nowhere To Run

SILHOUETTE·INTIMATE·MOMENTS®

Published by Silhouette Books New York

America's Publisher of Contemporary Romance

SILHOUETTE BOOKS
300 East 42nd St., New York, N.Y. 10017

NOWHERE TO RUN

ISBN: 0-373-07410-7

First Silhouette Books printing December 1991

Printed in the U.S.A.

MARY ANNE WILSON

fell in love with reading at age ten when she discovered *Pride and Prejudice*. A year later, she knew she had to be a writer when she found herself writing a new ending for *A Tale of Two Cities*. A true romantic, she had Sydney Carton rescued, and he lived happily ever after.

Though she's a native of Canada, she now lives in California with her husband and three children, a six-toed black cat who believes he's Hungarian and five timid Dobermans, who welcome any and all strangers. And she's writing happy endings for her own books.

For Sharon DiMeglio—
a good friend who listens, shares, and
doesn't dispute a writer's basic need to
go to two or three movies on a Friday.
Thanks.

Prologue

Lyndsey Cole's overriding emotion on the last Friday of October was relief that she was finally free. After months of wondering if it would ever happen, if she could make it happen, she had a new life, a good life, and on her terms.

It was late afternoon when she drove her small blue sedan off the Seattle street and into the underground parking garage for her apartment that overlooked Puget Sound. She knew the price she'd have to pay for freedom and peace of mind. She'd have to spend the rest of her life on her own. She'd never allow herself to depend on, or trust, anyone again. But she'd be safe.

She drove slowly, past the mostly empty parking spaces in the cavernous area, then slipped into her designated slot against the back wall. She turned her car off, then for a moment she sat in the silence, acknowledging one of the bonuses of her new life—a peace she'd never known before that seemed to seep into her soul.

She had faced the past and put it behind her. Rob Peters, with his false smiles and horrible anger, was safely in that past. Similarly, her childhood memories could have been those of a stranger. She was no longer that only child of career diplomats who had spent most of her childhood in boarding schools. A child who had been so lonely she had made up imaginary friends. And she was no longer the young woman who had married for all the wrong reasons, who had never been able to please her husband or deal with the emotional and physical pain he had given her.

She dropped her keys in her pocket, then glanced up at the rearview mirror, catching a glimpse of her own reflection there. She felt a momentary jolt at the sight of her new short feathery cut. For as long as she could remember, she'd had long blond hair framing her heart-shaped face, but she liked this now. It made her feel free, the way the contacts had made her feel free.

At the thought of her new contacts she sighed, then touched the frame of her glasses with the tip of her forefinger. She'd been in such a hurry to get to work yesterday morning that she'd torn one of her contacts. They had freed her from not only the physical weight of the thick lenses, but also the emotional weight of a child who had worn glasses since first grade. Now she had to wait until Monday morning to pick up the new lens her doctor had promised to have for her then.

Monday couldn't come soon enough for her, she thought, then she opened the door and got out. As she reached back in to get her purse off the seat, she was stunned by someone rushing up behind her and grabbing her by her upper arm. And her new life was shattered into a million pieces. Rob had found her.

With blinding speed, he was jerking her backward and out of the car with such force that her head snapped painfully to one side. She tried to suck in air, she tried to scream, but any sound was cut off by a hand clamping over her mouth and nose. Then the old Lyndsey was back, frantically trying to figure out how to placate him, knowing this was all her fault. Why had she been foolish enough to think she could ever be free of the man?

"He's going to kill me," she thought with numbing certainty. "He's really going to kill me this time." The horrible struggle of leaving him, of living at the shelter, of finally getting a divorce and leaving Dallas, had all been for nothing. Rob had made good on the threats he'd made when he'd found her at the shelter two days before the divorce had become final.

"You'll never get away from me, Lyndsey, never. I'll find you and you'll be sorry. I'll make you regret you were ever born."

She grasped at her determination to survive, the thing that had kept her going when she'd decided to escape from Rob and their marriage. No, she wasn't going to let him win. Her resolve never to take his abuse and be his victim again came to the forefront. Raw anger, which seemed to explode inside her, released a surge of adrenaline that gave her the strength to try and break free. As he dragged her backward, she lurched sideways, but his hold faltered for only a moment before he had her again, this time even tighter.

His arm circled her middle, trapping her with such strength that pain shot through her ribs and chest, and his hand on her mouth blocked her breathing. "This isn't fair!" she wanted to yell, and she fought against him, flailing her arms and legs, feeling contact with her heel against his leg.

He grunted, then threw her forward against her car. Her outstretched hands struck the cold metal, the impact jarring her arms and shoulders. But before she could run, before she could think of what her life would have been like if she'd never met Rob Peters and been stupid enough to believe in love and trust, she was spun around.

In that instant, her world became one of terror and fiery pain that filled every part of her body and soul.

Chapter 1

"I have an emergency interrupt for this telephone number. Will you relinquish the line?" the operator asked.

R. J. Tyler had been on the phone for the past hour with another psychiatrist, and he was more than willing to break the contact. As it was, the unexpected call had left him with less than an hour to get to the airport and make his flight out to Chicago.

"Of course, operator," he said, then spoke to the other doctor. "I'll be back from Chicago in a week. Give me a call at my office then, and we can arrange a consultation."

"Thanks, I'll do that. See you then," the man said, then he hung up.

R.J. put the receiver in the cradle and sank back on the couch in the darkened living room of his apartment on the southern edge of Seattle. Before he could do more than wonder who was making the emergency cut-in, the phone rang. He reached for it and said, "Dr. Tyler."

"Doctor. This is Officer Donner. Detective Mac-Clain asked me to call you."

R.J. had expected the call to be from one of the doctors he'd been working with to form a victim's rights group, not someone calling for his brother-in-law, Russ MacClain. If Russ was anything beyond one of the best detectives on the Seattle Police Department, he was a direct man who would never have a second party call for him. "What's going on?"

"Detective MacClain is in his car on his way to your place. He asked me to get through and tell you he'll be there any minute."

He looked at his watch. Ten o'clock. His flight was set for eleven. "I'm on my way out the door. I'm catching an eleven o'clock flight out to Chicago. Tell Russ to call me there at—"

"Sir, he needs to see you right away. He said to tell you it's an emergency."

The doorbell chimed, followed by a sharp rapping on the front door. "I think he's here now," R.J. said, then hung up.

He crossed the softly lit room to the foyer, stepped around his suitcase sitting on the carpet by the door, and reached for the knob. When he pulled the door open, Russ was in the hallway. The large man wore a rumpled brown suit that was almost the same color as the slightly shaggy hair that framed his square face.

It was always hard for R.J. to remember that Russ was only two years older than himself, for at forty-three, he had a decided air of weariness that clung to him like a second skin and added years to his appearance. Despite the fact that he was the same height as R.J. at six feet,

Russ seemed larger, with his massive shoulders, huge hands and a way of walking that looked as if each step could shake the world. He was an imposing man, and that only enhanced his ability to deal with the criminal part of the population of Seattle.

"Thank God you're here," Russ said as he strode past R.J., his deep voice breathless. He'd probably forgone the slow elevator and walked up the flights of stairs to the apartment.

R.J. closed the door, then turned. Russ stood by the entry to the living room. "I'm on my way to Chicago for the conference on victim's rights," R.J. explained. He glanced at his wristwatch. "And if I'm not out of here in five minutes, I'll miss my flight. What's this all about?"

"I need to talk to you," Russ said, his large frame vaguely blurred by the shadows at his back.

R.J. leaned against the door and knew that his brother-in-law wasn't a capricious man. This had to be important. "What's wrong?"

"We found the fourth victim of the B & B Strangler two hours ago."

Russ was the kind of cop who lived his work, and R.J. had watched the Strangler case take its toll on him. Blond, blue-eyed women in Seattle were terrified, and the press was having a field day with their coverage. They'd even coined the name that gave the killer a sort of notoriety that infuriated Russ. "Give them a nickname and they try to live up to it," he always said. Nickname or not, Russ was after this guy, and he needed a break in the case, not another woman dead. "The same MO?" R.J. asked.

"Yeah, blond, blue-eyed, in her twenties, alone, beaten and choked. But this time the killer made a mistake, a fatal mistake."

R.J. stood straight. "What?"

"This one's alive. She took a hard blow to the head and was choked. She's got a concussion, and she's unconscious, but the doctors are optimistic that she'll pull out of it soon."

"How did she survive?"

"Luck. Fate. His stupidity. Maybe he was scared off before he made sure he'd killed her. Maybe he got sloppy. I don't know. What we do know is that he abducted her and took her south of here to an isolated field off a side road. Same pattern as before. But this time the victim was rescued. It seems a salesman got lost, his car overheated, and he headed across the field to get help. He heard her moan, went to investigate and found her in a shallow ditch. He didn't see anyone else around. What counts is that she's alive and can finger the killer when she regains consciousness."

"What a break for you."

"For us."

"What?"

"I want you in on it," Russ said.

R.J. narrowed his eyes, then deliberately reached for the light switch and flooded the small foyer in brightness. He stared directly at Russ and said bluntly, "I wish you luck with the case, but count me out. I'm heading for Chicago, and I'll be gone for at least a week."

Russ rocked forward on the balls of his feet. "I want you to cancel, R.J. I want you on the payroll. I want you to be there when the victim regains consciousness. I want you to be the one to help her deal with what she's been through, and I want you to be the one to make sure she's the best damned witness we can have.''

R.J. felt his whole being tighten at what Russ was saying. ''No,'' he said bluntly. ''I can't.'' He walked past Russ into the living room. Without turning on the lights, he crossed the darkened room to the windows that looked down at the city and out to Puget Sound in the distance.

The light from the foyer reflected in the window panes and the glare reflected back on R.J. For an instant he saw himself clearly. An angular jaw, deep-set hazel eyes, slightly shaggy brown hair shot with streaks of silver, and a sports coat and pale shirt that were a blur in the glass. Every once in a while when he caught his reflection without being prepared, he was struck by how the outward man could remain the same while the inner man underwent tremendous change.

No mirror or glass could show the real changes in him. Nothing could show the fact that he knew he could never be the man he'd been three years ago. And he'd never be the psychiatrist he'd been then, either. He flicked his gaze past his image to the night outside as he listened to Russ moving into the room.

''I wish you hadn't come here,'' R.J. said without turning.

''I had to, R.J. You're the only one who can pull this off.''

The city lights far below blurred. ''I can give you the names of some good doctors who can help you.''

''I want you. I've seen what you've done in the past. You've pioneered victim's rights programs. You've worked with people who've gone through hell, and you've helped them come back and face what they had to face. You've made it possible for them to get on a witness stand and put away people who've done unspeakable things to them. You've worked miracles before, and I need one from you now."

Miracles? There were no miracles in this world, especially not in his life, and Russ should know that better than anyone. He turned to the large man who was a stark shadow backed by the glare of light from the foyer. "That's all in the past, Russ, and that's exactly where my talents are."

Russ exhaled harshly. "I don't buy that."

"You don't have to. I know it's the truth, and I know I can't do it for you."

Russ stared at R.J. hard, then he said something that R.J. never expected. "You owe me, R.J., and I'm calling in the markers."

That statement had the impact of a fist in his stomach. His friendship with Russ had never been based on a points system—I did for you, so you have to do for me. And it bothered R.J. that it had come down to that now.

"We both know what's between us, R.J., what's always been there, even before Maddy was in the picture, before all the grief you went through. Hell, the grief we both went through."

R.J. knew and he remembered. Russ and he had met in boot camp and served together during the Vietnam War. Then, when they'd been released, he'd come back to Seattle with Russ for a few weeks. Those few weeks had turned into a lifetime when he'd met Russ's sister, Madeline, and fallen in love with her. From that moment on their lives had been joined irrevocably, as irrevocably as Maddy had become R.J.'s life.

And three years ago when that life had been shattered, the psychiatrist had been unable to help himself. That's when Russ had been there, breaking through

R.J.'s drunken haze, working past his own grieving for his only sister to help R.J. get on with his life.

R.J. had gone back to work, but not back to the one-on-one therapy sessions. No, R.J. had narrowed his work to consultations with police departments all over the country, and addressing conferences on victim's rights. No more one-on-one sessions.

He shook his head sharply. "I never thought you'd do this to me."

"I never thought a killer would be terrorizing Seattle like this." Russ shrugged, his massive shoulders moving sharply. "Bottom line is I need you to help me."

R.J. turned to the windows and spoke the stark truth. "I can't do it anymore, Russ."

"Sure you can. I wouldn't have come for you if I thought you couldn't help." Russ inhaled, then released the breath in a rush. "I understand where you're coming from. I know what you've gone through since Maddy died."

No, you don't, R.J. wanted to scream at him, but kept silent as he pressed his fingertips against the cold glass of the window.

"You know how much I loved Maddy, R.J. Damn it, she was my sister, all the family I had except you. But it's been three years since she died, and you have a talent, a God-given talent for helping trauma victims face life. Maddy would want you to be using it."

"I'm working. You know that, and if you weren't here, I'd be on my way to Chicago right now instead of missing my flight."

"You'd be on your way to give a lecture, to discuss abstract ideas. That's not what I meant. Maybe I should have worded things differently. You can help people, and Lyndsey Cole needs your help."

"Lyndsey Cole?"

"Our survivor."

"You I.D.'d her?"

"Yeah. We found keys in her pocket and traced a tag from apartments over the Sound. She's Lyndsey Cole, and she's all we've got. I need you to be there for her when she regains consciousness." Russ hesitated. "Just talk to her. Give me something to help her deal with the attack. Do that, and the Seattle Police Department will pay you well, plus they'll buy you a first-class ticket to Chicago."

"You know it's not the money."

"You're right. It's life and death."

R.J. closed his eyes. Life and death. He knew both too well. And Lyndsey Cole would have to face both of them when she regained consciousness. Maybe it was the years of practice, but he found in that moment that he couldn't just turn his back and walk away. "Maybe I could put off going to Chicago for a day. I don't have to give my speech until Sunday. But that's all the time I can give you."

"I'll take it," Russ said quickly.

He opened his eyes and turned back to face Russ. "All right. I'll come. I'll be there. I'll talk to her, and then she's all yours."

"She's at Blair Memorial." Russ turned to walk to the door. "Come on. I'll drive."

Twenty-four hours later, R.J. wasn't on a flight out to Chicago, but in a room on the tenth floor of Blair Memorial Hospital, and Lyndsey Cole still hadn't regained consciousness. And in those hours of watching and waiting, he'd found out he'd been right. He wasn't equipped to deal with the intensity of his reaction to the sight of a victim.

Compassion had always been an intricate part of his work. And he had been driven by the need to set victims' lives in order, to help them on the road to a successful recovery from damage done to them by violence. Now he couldn't face it—he didn't have it in him to deal with this anymore.

He had to take a deep breath as he crossed the room where the only sounds were the monitoring systems by the narrow, rail-sided bed. Foolishly he'd let himself forget about this gut-level pain that could leave him breathless when he faced the end product of violence. It shouldn't have surprised him that the pain hadn't lessened any during his absence, and it hadn't lessened during his frequent trips in to see the patient.

He checked the monitor and picked up her chart, scanning it, seeing it was unchanged since an hour ago when he'd been in here. The prognosis was still the same—the sooner she regained consciousness, the less chance of complications. And the less chance of other women being killed, R.J. thought as he slipped the chart back on its hook at the end of the bed. Then he came around to the side of the bed and reached out to the rail, slowly curling his strong fingers around the cold metal. Narrowing his eyes to soften the impact, he looked directly at Lyndsey Cole.

She seemed incredibly tiny and delicate, with fine hair that came close to the color of corn silk ripened in the summer. It was cut short, and it feathered over a bandage on her right temple. R.J. winced at the way her left cheekbone and eye were swollen and bruised. And her pale lips were still puffy from the tightness of the gag the killer had used on her.

"She sustained a blow to the temple probably when she fell after being struck in the face," the doctor had said. *"It looks as if he subdued her by knocking her out with a punch to the face, bound and gagged her, then attempted to strangle her."*

R.J.'s eyes dropped to the deep, ugly ring of raw, bruised skin where the nylon cord had cut into her slender neck. A necklace that held no beauty. *"Same murder weapon, a nylon cord, but the kind you can buy in any variety store. Generic, really generic,"* Russ had told him. Then he looked at the bracelets of bruises on either wrist.

He'd been struck the first time how slender, how delicately boned Lyndsey was, although she was probably average height, five foot five or so. She wasn't busty or voluptuous in any way, yet decidedly feminine. His eyes traveled over the outline of her body under the light sheet, from her surprisingly long legs, to the gentle flaring of her hips, her flat stomach, then the swelling of her breasts. Small and high, her breasts barely moved the cotton of the sheets as each shallow breath was taken in, then released.

He stared at her. What had she looked like two days ago? Had men turned to look at her when she passed by? Had she been able to stir them and attract them with just a look or a gesture? Had they perceived her the way he had moments ago? Had they wanted to protect her, or lie with her and love her, to feel her cuddled against them in the shadows of the night?

R.J. felt a sudden rush of heat under his skin and looked quickly away, stunned at the sudden course his mind had taken. It shocked, confused and angered him. He'd never looked at a patient with anything other than professional concern and compassion. In the past few years he hadn't looked at *any* woman like this.

He closed his eyes, wondering if this had been even more of a mistake than he'd first thought. Then he knew that it had to be a by-product of this case. Everyone was on edge, filled with anxiety and worry. That put everything into perspective. This wasn't a normal time. Hell, he didn't even know what normal was anymore and probably wouldn't recognize it if it came up and hit him in the face.

He opened his eyes and looked at Lyndsey, and he had a thought he'd had so many times over the years—what possessed one human being to do this to another human being? Even as a psychiatrist who was supposed to understand the workings of humans, he had no answers, only questions. What had Lyndsey done, or what had someone perceived she'd done, that had made him want to kill her? Was it just because she'd been born blond and blue-eyed? Had it all been governed by that flimsy premise? Was life just a series of chances engineered by the capricious whims of fate?

If Lyndsey hadn't been alone yesterday in her parking structure, she wouldn't be here now. He wouldn't be looking down at her filled with frustration that the concussion kept her from waking and telling what had happened to her. She would have escaped.

On the other hand, if he hadn't taken the time to talk to his colleague on the phone before leaving for the airport, and if Russ had come to the apartment five minutes later, he wouldn't be here at the hospital now. He wouldn't have let Russ talk him into doing this, and he would have been in Chicago at a safe distance from this situation. He would have escaped.

From nowhere came the memory of the man he'd been before Maddy had died. He hadn't had thoughts of escape then, but he'd had a willingness to work with a vengeance for days and weeks, sometimes months, to get victims of violent crimes to fight back. He'd helped them want to live and get on with their lives, and to do whatever they could to get their attackers arrested and convicted.

That man was him, before he'd found out on a personal level how easy it was to want to stop living. And he hadn't had to endure physical violence. Just emotional devastation—losing the one woman he'd truly loved.

He had a stunning thought that had only flitted through his mind earlier. Did someone love Lyndsey? What was Lyndsey Cole's past? The police hadn't been able to find any family or friends, but he wondered if there was a man out there going crazy because she'd disappeared. Was the agony of not knowing what had happened to her killing him?

Agony wouldn't begin to describe what someone who loved this woman would feel when they saw her like this. They wouldn't know it for a while, but they were blessed. They wouldn't lose her completely. There would be time to say words that should have been said, to tie up the loose ends of their lives. Some people never got that chance.

He started to turn away, needing to leave, shaken by a wave of bitterness, frustration and regret that washed over him, but stopped when Lyndsey moaned softly. He looked back at her and jolted when he saw her eyelids tremble, then still. So, it had begun. The awakening. The coma was getting less deep, with rapid eye movement showing the presence of a true dream state.

When she moaned again, he hesitated, then touched her forehead by the bandage. Her skin felt cool and clammy under his fingertips and as delicate as parchment. He looked at her hands lying by her side on the stark white of the hospital linen; her left hand had an IV fastened to the back with tape. He avoided looking at the bruises on her wrists and noticed her hands, graceful, with slender fingers and short oval nails, but with knuckles that were bruised and cut. She'd fought. She hadn't gone quietly. A survivor.

The hands of an artist, Russ had told him earlier. He glanced at her left hand, and for the first time saw a very pale circle on her ring finger. He'd been so distracted by her injuries that he hadn't noticed the evidence that there was probably a husband or a fiancé out there... somewhere. And the attacker had taken the ring.

"Hey, R.J..."

He looked to his right as Russ strode quickly into the room. The door shut quietly behind the large man. "Anything yet?" he asked in a hushed voice as he came closer to the bed and looked past R.J. at Lyndsey.

"There's some REM, so she's sliding into a true dream state," he said. "It's just a matter of time before she opens her eyes."

"I wish to God we had time, but you know we don't." Russ stared hard at the woman. "This animal's got a pattern of sorts, with the calm between the killings getting shorter and shorter. The first was three months from the second, and this was just three weeks from the last. God knows when the next one will be, or if the next woman will be this lucky."

R.J. turned from the bed and went across the green-and-white room to the single window. Being lucky was all in the opinion of the person using the term. He stared out at the gathering dusk settling over the city below, making Puget Sound a dark smudge in the distance. Sometimes surviving wasn't being lucky at all. "Have you found any relatives yet?" he asked, trying to side-track his own thoughts.

"None," Russ said from behind him.

"Did you notice that she used to wear a wedding ring, or at least an engagement ring?"

"Yeah. Still has the tan line on her finger—faint, but it's there."

R.J. stared hard at the city lights far below the tenth-floor room. "There has to be someone out there look-ing for her, Russ."

"Not that we've found. She seems to have been living in the apartment alone. Only been there a month or so. No prints but hers, no personal papers, not even an ad-dress book or phone book. She's working. We found her purse in her car and a hire-in slip in it, along with a pay stub. The company, a graphic arts company, is closed for the weekend and we haven't been able to locate the owner.

"Her apartment manager says she told him she's been traveling so she didn't have a former street address, just a post office box in Dallas. We're checking the social security number from her pay stub, but that could be fake." He paused, then added, "I've got a gut feeling she's deliberately getting lost, deliberately wiping out her past."

"A criminal background?" R.J. asked, even though he had great difficulty seeing Lyndsey as a criminal.

"Not that we know of. Her prints don't show any-where, not local, state or federal. She's clean as a whis-tle."

''But everyone has a past. Someone has to be asking questions.''

''There've been no reports filed about a missing person with her description.''

R.J. closed his eyes. ''A picture wouldn't do any good, not with what's happened to her.''

He heard Russ crossing the room, then he was by his side holding out a three-by-five color picture. ''We have a picture. It was in a side pocket of a makeup case in her purse, along with two thousand dollars in cash. This is Lyndsey Cole.''

Chapter 2

R.J. took the photo Russ held out to him, then looked down at it, a colored print with dog-eared corners. Lyndsey looked as if she might have been fifteen or sixteen in it, and she was standing on an expanse of silvery beach with an older couple on either side of her.

The man was just inches taller than Lyndsey, heavy-set, with a mustache, staring right into the camera and looking out of place in a dark, three-piece suit. The woman was shorter and slender, with curly pale hair and wearing a blue dress that would have been more appropriate for an afternoon tea. She looked downward, as if studying her feet.

R.J. couldn't tell where it might have been taken. He flipped the photo over and saw faded writing: "Mary, Lyndsey and Robert, summer vacation."

He turned it back over. Even as a teenager in a very modest one-piece bathing suit, Lyndsey Cole had been pretty. Pale hair fell straight from a center part to well past her shoulders. Wide-set eyes were narrowed from the brilliance of the sun, and her lips were lifted in a smile.

Then he realized that something basic was wrong with the photo. Lyndsey wasn't touching either person or being touched by them. She held a towel in one hand and tinted glasses in the other. It was as if a peculiar scene of isolation had been frozen for all time in that picture—three people with no contact by touch or look. It made him wonder if Lyndsey might have been as alone then as she was now.

He handed the picture back to Russ and looked back out at the night. "If they're her parents and they're still alive, they have to be looking for her. Isn't there some way you can get that picture out?"

"No. Once it's out, her name's out, and the killer finds out everything. Let her be just as anonymous as she seems to want to be, a victim we're waiting to ID, a victim who's in a deep coma. That way the killer doesn't think she's a threat—just yet, and we buy some precious time."

It made perfect sense, yet R.J. couldn't let it go. "But if her family's looking for her?"

"They aren't." Russ cut him off abruptly. "No reports, no calls, no questions. We even checked with the Dallas PD. No one's looking for her."

R.J. found that hard to believe. The girl in the picture wouldn't slip through this life unnoticed, without someone caring. The pale circle on her finger only underscored that. "Did the guy ever rob his other victims?"

"Not that we know of. And I don't think this was a robbery at all. He didn't touch her money—two grand. I'd guess she took that ring off herself. Maybe that's why she's living alone in a small apartment in a strange city without a paper trail to her past.''

"I guess stranger things have happened."

"Life's strange, R.J., but it goes on."

Life goes on. The sun always rises. Time heals all wounds, and Lyndsey Cole beat the odds. She was the only one of the four victims to survive. R.J. took a deep breath before he turned and saw Russ back by the side of the hospital bed slipping the picture into his inside pocket.

Then R.J. let his gaze slide past the large man to Lyndsey, her slender figure covered by the thin sheets, the IV in the back of her hand, the monitors softly beeping, and he felt his throat constrict. Then he took a breath and went to the foot of the bed. "Maybe she'll wake up tonight."

"It can't be too soon for me," Russ said, then asked, "Do you want me to send in someone to spell you for a while?"

"Not yet," R.J. said as he glanced at his watch. "It's just going on eleven o'clock. I'll stay here awhile longer."

"All right. I've got to make some calls on the phone by the elevators, but I'll let you know before I leave." With one last pained look at Lyndsey, Russ shook his head, then silently left the room.

R.J. watched the door shut behind Russ, then he heard Lyndsey moan softly and he turned. Without hesitating, he reached out to her, touching her cheek. He knew about being alone, and he wanted her to have some sense of his presence. Maybe it would help her ease into consciousness if she knew someone was here for her. His fingertips barely made contact with her cool skin, when she turned and moaned again.

"Lyndsey?" he said in a whisper as he bent over her, aware of each slow, shallow breath she took and the eye movement behind her closed lids. "Lyndsey?"

Lyndsey was snatched from nothingness and plunged into the middle of a strange, disjointed dream. She was driving into the underground garage at the apartment, going down the ramp into the softly lit concrete structure, and all around her was a strange voice saying her name in gentle whispers. But she didn't know who was speaking or why she sensed the voice rather than actually heard it.

Then her car was stopping, she was reaching to turn off the key, and without warning, terror seemed to be everywhere. One part of her could think rationally about her eyes being closed, about lying on something firm and cool, yet she was experiencing a terror that was all-encompassing. And she felt deathly cold, except for a single spot of warmth on her face. Heat seemed to come from that spot in waves, and in some way she felt as if she was connected with life. Not with death.

Death. Rob, he'd tried to kill her. He'd found her. He'd done what he said he would do. But she didn't think she was dead. No, she was in a bed, hurting in every part of her body, very much alive. Somewhere above her a low, insistent voice was saying her name over and over again, and the heat on her cheek seemed to be connected with the sound of the voice.

"Lyndsey? Lyndsey?"

Then she knew the heat came from being touched, and the voice belonged to a man. Not Rob. He had never touched her with such gentleness after the first few months. But where was he? He had to be close by. He'd be waiting. The need to run ripped through her. Rob was

never going to let her go. Never. He'd threatened her.
He'd told her she couldn't run. She'd tried, God, she'd
tried, but he'd found her. All she could think of was
running again and never stopping.

Then she felt a slow stroking on her cheek, and the
voice came closer. Don't let him hurt me again, she
wanted to beg this man with the gentle voice. Don't let
him kill me. Then as if the man understood, as if he
could read her mind, he was saying, "You're going to be
all right. You're safe now."

She wanted to tell this man Rob would never leave,
that she'd never be safe, but when she tried to make a
sound, instant and fiery pain exploded in her throat and
her ribs tightened horribly.

"Lyndsey, Lyndsey," the voice said from just above
her. "Fight it. That's it. Wake up. Open your eyes. You
can do it, Lyndsey. Just open your eyes," the stranger
persisted, closer now, so close she could feel the brush of
his warm breath on her face. "Don't give up. Fight it.
Fight it."

Maybe this man would be different, maybe he could
do what no one had been able to do up to now, not even
Estelle at the shelter or the Dallas police with their restraining orders. If she could make him understand
about Rob, if she could make him believe her and help
her, maybe this time would be different.

"That's it. That's it. Don't drift away. Fight it," the
man was saying. "Fight, Lyndsey."

She concentrated, and with monumental effort she
managed to make her eyelids open a fraction of an inch,
enough to see brightness all around.

"That's it. Look at me," the voice encouraged her.
"Look at me."

She blinked, the brightness gradually easing into a world of blurred lights and darks, smears of green, white and brown. She blinked again, but knew she wouldn't see things any more clearly for the effort it took to try and focus. She couldn't see more than a foot in front of her without her contacts or her glasses.

"Pl-please..." she croaked, and her throat constricted painfully. She instinctively lifted her hand to try and ease the pain that brought tears to her eyes. But the stranger had her hand, easing it back gently onto the coolness of the cotton by her side. "G-glasses..." she whispered.

He let her go, and for a minute she thought he'd read her mind again, that he knew she needed her glasses. She caught blurry movement over her, then to her right. As she tried to shift a bit to watch it, the slight action shot more pain up her neck into her head, and down into her shoulders, making her gasp.

"Don't move," the voice was saying from a distance, then it was coming closer. "Lie still."

Then the man was back, a blurred image leaning over her, and she had a wrenching thought that she might have been fooled, that this man with the gentle voice was really Rob playacting. She knew how good he was at playing a role—the concerned husband, the contrite husband, the loving husband. None of those roles had been real. Had he fooled her again?

"Lyndsey, you're going to be all right." Then she knew how wrong she was. This person's voice was low and soft and brought more tears to her eyes. She needed to see this man. "Glasses..." she managed to say against the pain. "I...I have...I..."

Something touched her lips. "Here. Take a drink," the man said. "Be careful, just let the water slip down your throat."

A straw. It didn't matter that the man had misunderstood, right then her need for water to soothe her throat was all-encompassing. She tried to form her lips around the straw, but she could barely manage to draw a small amount of water into her mouth to touch the cottony dryness there. Then the liquid trickled down to the fire that seemed to engulf her neck. Her muscles constricted horribly at first, but began to ease as the coolness washed downward. With a great effort she managed to swallow twice.

"Good, good," the man murmured, then moved out of Lyndsey's line of vision, and she didn't try to look at him this time. Weakly she closed her eyes and touched her tongue to her lips. They felt strange, puffy, tender, unresponsive. "Who?" she got out in a weak croak.

The man understood this time and said, "I'm R. J. Tyler. I'm helping the Seattle Police Department."

Police? At the beginning of her nightmare with Rob she would have been thankful for the police, but not now. She knew how limited they were in what they could do for her with their restraining orders and empty threats to Rob. It was better for her to leave, to disappear again. She opened her eyes to the brightness that made her eyes ache and her head throb horribly. If this overwhelming weariness would go away and if she could just get up—

Without a word the man moved off to the side, his footsteps striking on tile. In the next instant the bright lights were gone. Only a soft side light lit the room of shadows and blurred shapes. "Th-thank you," Lyndsey said with a sigh as the man came back to her.

"Do you know where you are, Lyndsey?"

She started to talk again, to tell him she only knew she was alive, but nothing would come this time.

"It's okay, don't talk. I know it's painful. Just blink your eyes once for yes, twice for no."

She blinked her eyes twice.

"You're in Blair Memorial Hospital. You have a concussion, and you've been unconscious since they brought you in twenty-four hours ago."

Twenty-four hours? A whole day. She didn't have time to listen to this man. She had to get out of here. She concentrated on feeling her body, her arms and legs, her hands and feet. Physically she hurt, but she sensed that she was in one piece, and she knew if she could find the energy, she could move. If she could just get up. "I...I have to..."

"All you have to do is get better. No one can get to you. You'll be all right. No broken bones. Nothing permanent. Just a lot of soreness and bruises and the concussion. But you're awake, and everyone's been waiting for this since they brought you in."

"Where...is...he?" she forced out past the pain.

"That's what we need you to tell us. You're our only clue, our only survivor."

Lyndsey didn't understand. What was he talking about. The only survivor? "What?"

"The others weren't as lucky as you are. For some reason, he left you alive. He must have thought he'd killed you when he left you in the field. A man who got lost found you and got help."

No, this was all wrong. Rob had done this to her. He'd tried to kill her but hadn't been able to follow through on it. Maybe he was the man they thought found her. Maybe he was nearby right now ready to finish what he'd started, or maybe he was telling lies and getting sympathy for himself. "She fell and I was helping her," he'd say, not that he'd found her by the road.

"I... don't... understand," she whispered hoarsely.

"What don't you understand?" he asked.

She touched her tongue to her lips and felt sore puffiness. "What did... he say?"

"The man who found you?"

She blinked once, not able to stand the pain of talking again.

"He got lost, had car trouble, and he was walking for help when he heard you moaning. He found you in a gully filled with thick ground cover and went for help. They airlifted you here."

No, Rob had found her in the garage, not in some field. "His name?"

"I don't know his name. The police questioned him, and let him go."

Let him go? God, her head hurt from trying to make sense of this. "Please... help me. I don't..." She tried to take in air, but the tightness in her ribs wouldn't let them expand completely.

"We are helping you. No one can get to you. You're in protective custody and are getting the best medical care. Until we catch the killer, you'll have police with you day and night."

Killer? But she wasn't dead. She had to move, to sit up, to run, to get away before Rob came back. But when she tried to lift her head, incredible pain shot through her, and she sank back into the bed. Tears burned her eyes, tears of frustration and fear. "No... Rob," she whispered, her words thick and slurred.

"He didn't rob you, at least you still have the money in your purse. I know this is horrible for you. But you're all we have. You're the only one who's seen the killer. You're the only hope we have of catching him.''

Lyndsey wanted to scream Rob's name at this man, to make him quit talking about some killer. But her lips felt unresponsive, and she couldn't force any more words past the tightness in her throat. She had never felt such weakness in her life or so much pain and discomfort. Tears slid silently down her cheeks, fear making her heart pound against her ribs.

"Lyndsey, listen to me," R.J. said softly very close to her. "This guy's killed three other women in Seattle. He's still out there, and unless we can stop him, he'll kill again."

She finally understood what he was talking about. They thought she'd been attacked by some killer. But she knew Rob had done this to her. He'd grabbed her as she'd gotten out of her car, then jerked her around so she had to look in his face. No, no, that wasn't right. She realized that wasn't right at all. She knew her attacker had been Rob, but there was no actual face in her memory. There was no memory beyond being spun around.

But it had to be Rob. Something told her that was the truth, yet she couldn't remember anything from that instant when she was jerked around until she woke here with this man telling her she'd survived an attack by some killer.

Her immediate instinct to trust this man and tell him about Rob died almost as quickly as it came to her. If Rob did this to her, no one could protect her from him. If it wasn't Rob, the police would be making contact with him to check, and one way or another, he'd find out where she was.

She felt her stomach churn with nausea. She'd awakened in the middle of a nightmare; her world had turned upside down. No matter what anyone thought, no matter that they talked about a killer, she knew what she had to do. She had to do what she'd done a month ago. Run. But this time she'd keep running until she knew Rob would never find her again.

Unexpectedly, R.J. touched her hand, and the shock of the contact made her pull away abruptly. Her gasp from the instant pain that shot up her arm and into her neck came out in a broken sob. Closing her eyes tightly, she took in a breath.

"I'm sorry. I know you're scared," R.J. said, not touching her again. "You've got every right to be. But everyone else in Seattle is scared, too. Right now, you need to have the doctor look at you, and I have to let the police know you're finally conscious and can tell them what they need to know."

"No," she said, opening her eyes to the world of blurred shapes and shadows. Not seeing clearly made this easier for her to say. "I...don't remember anything. I...I need to get out of here."

R.J. stared at Lyndsey, at her lashes spiked by tears and her face as white as the cotton of the pillowcase under her head. Her eyes, which had stunned him with their incredible blueness in that instant she opened them, were bright with more tears. "What are you talking about?" he asked.

Her lips worked, then she whispered hoarsely, "I need to...to get out of here. Please help me."

"That's why I'm here. You're safe here. This section of the floor is protected. There's an officer outside your door, and one spotted by the elevators and another at the nurses' station. Now tell me what you meant when you said you don't remember anything."

Her right hand curled so tightly into a fist that her knuckles were bloodless. "I don't remember." She touched her tongue to her swollen bottom lip. "I can't...remember anything."

He could hardly take in what she said. Yet he knew he should have expected something like this—selective amnesia, or plain denial so she wouldn't have to deal with it. Whatever was going on with her, he had to approach this carefully and try to get to the truth. "Tell me, what *do* you remember, Lyndsey?"

"The garage...my car...s-someone behind..." She closed her eyes, and the breath she took in was jerky, making her body tremble under the sheets. "Nothing...black...then I was here."

"You said 'he' before."

She paled even more, scrunching her eyes tightly closed. "I don't...know," she whispered. "I guess...I thought..." She exhaled on a shuddering sob. "I have to leave. I can't tell you anything. I just have to get out of here."

He ignored her last words. "Maybe you've lost some memory, a segment of time. That's called 'patch memory loss.' That's normal. Trauma can do it. Fear can do it. Things we can't deal with. Your mind protects you by letting you hide from what you've gone through. That's a completely normal reaction."

She kept her eyes closed. "Normal?"

"Predictable might be a better word."

Her lids fluttered, then she was looking at him, her eyes softly blurred, her pupils oddly dilated, probably the aftermath of the concussion. "I can't tell you anything. I...I really can't," she breathed unsteadily.

He looked down at her. Her feathered hair was a pale contrast to the deep bruising on her skin. "Maybe not now, but later. First, you need to have the doctor check you and make sure things are all right. Then we'll see what you can remember.''

She frowned, drawing the discolored skin by her eyes at an odd angle with the bandage. "It's blank. There's nothing," she insisted.

"You said you remember driving into your apartment parking structure?"

"Yes," she whispered.

"Then what?"

"Just...there, getting out of my car." She swallowed hard. "A hand on my arm, then nothing."

"Are you sure you didn't see your attacker at all?"

"I don't remember," she whispered, then looked away from R.J., her gaze going past him to some spot on the far wall.

"Lyndsey, think. When the killer touched you, you turned, didn't you? It's instinctive to turn to someone who's threatening you. The killer—"

Her blue eyes came back to meet his gaze, a frown narrowing them, as if Lyndsey couldn't quite bear to focus on reality. "Killer?"

"The person who did this to you."

"But I'm alive."

He braced himself, then plunged in with both feet. "Three women he found before you aren't alive. Do you remember hearing about the B & B Strangler?"

She paled even more, the bruises and discolorations on her face so vivid that he wished he could blot out his last words. But he knew he couldn't. Nothing could soften the emotional impact of what she'd gone through. But she could keep other women from experiencing the same thing. And she either knew everything, or she had answers hidden somewhere in her mind.

"That...that's who...?" Her voice trailed off, but her eyes never left R.J.'s face.

"It looks that way."

"But I was in the garage, in the car, and..."

He let the reality of the cold metal of the rail under his hands keep him focused. "It looks as if he found you in the garage, that you struggled there by your car. That's why you had to have seen his face."

The room fell silent as Lyndsey seemed to sink even further into the pillows with a shuddering sigh. Her lips trembled, and her right hand grabbed at the blanket, twisting the fabric in a death grip.

"Couldn't it...be someone else?"

"Who?" he asked.

"I don't know." She closed her eyes, and tears slipped silently down her cheeks. "I don't know. But why me?"

"You fit the basic description of the others, but there's no way to understand the mind of someone like that. Maybe it was all chance. Maybe you just happened to be in the wrong place at the wrong time. But you were lucky. You survived."

"But, I...I..." she stammered.

When she began to tremble, he acted instinctively and reached out for her to touch her clenched hand. He wasn't prepared for the way her eyes flew open and she pulled away from the contact. She drew her hand tightly to her breast and gasped, "Don't...don't touch me." She took a shuddering breath. "Just help me get out of here."

"You're in mild shock, Lyndsey. What you need is rest and help to deal with this," he said as he drew his hand back. But as he said the words, he knew what she needed. She needed someone to hold her and love her, someone to anchor her in this world until she could make some sense out of what she'd gone through. "Let me contact someone for you and get them here to help you."

She looked right at him, and for a moment he could have sworn he saw raw fear in her eyes. Then it was gone, and she spoke in a flat voice. "There is no one to contact."

There was no emotion in her voice, yet the words broke his heart. It wasn't right for this woman to be alone in the world. It wasn't right that all she had was a psychiatrist who wished he was in Chicago and a police force that saw her as a means to an end.

She was lying there very still, watching him, waiting. And he had no idea what to do. So he said words that were kind, words that were true but impersonal. "You can't leave, yet. You're too weak, and you have to be monitored because of the concussion. You need rest, and you need help to deal with what happened."

And while he spoke to her, while he looked into the blueness of her eyes, he was stunned by the realization that he wanted to be the one to hold her and push her pain away. And he was just as shocked that he felt that way about a woman again. He thought those feelings had died with Maddy. But they hadn't, and this stranger with pale hair and huge eyes was making him feel things he wasn't so sure he could deal with right now.

Chapter 3

With R.J. just a blur above her, Lyndsey focused on his voice saying that she was trapped here. She tried to take a breath, to regroup and get past her pain and confusion. A killer or Rob? Someone had left her for dead. He'd tried to take her life. He'd beaten her. She tried to hold back tears, knowing tears never made things better.

She didn't remember any of what happened to her after she got out of the car. It was darkness, blankness, as if she'd ceased living from the moment her attacker had spun her around until she woke to hear this man's voice saying her name.

She steeled herself, pulling as much air as she could into her lungs, then releasing it slowly. She made herself focus on what she had to do. She had to get out of the hospital. As long as there was a chance Rob knew she was here, she couldn't stay.

Her head hurt, throbbing with a life of its own, and she had to swallow twice to control threatening nausea. What was worse? A stranger trying to kill her because of how she looked, or Rob finding her and making good on his threat? If she could get to a telephone, she could find out where Rob was right now. "You have to help me," she breathed.

Then she sensed R.J. was closer, bending over her, the scent of heat mingled with mellow after-shave was all around her, and she was terrified that he'd touch her again. Touching was something she'd come to hate, something she didn't want or need.

But he didn't touch her. Instead, he spoke softly. "That's why I'm here. To help you."

For a moment she wanted his help desperately, she wanted to tell him about Rob and beg him to help her escape. But she couldn't get the words past her lips. She knew she couldn't tell him anything. If Rob did this, he'd be back. The police wouldn't be able to stop him. And if he didn't, if it was some killer and the police knew about Rob, they'd contact him, then he'd know where she was. She wouldn't believe promises that they wouldn't talk to him. She knew better than to believe anyone's promises. She couldn't take that chance that they'd find Rob and lead him to her here.

"If... you want to help..." She touched her tongue to her lips. "Get me out of here."

"I can't do that."

"Why? I'm not under arrest, am I?"

"Of course you aren't. But you need protection. You said there's no one to help you. Maybe if you had family it would be different, but for now, you need to be here."

The word "family" was an anachronism to Lyndsey. She'd never felt part of one, not when she was at the boarding schools while her parents were at their posts overseas. And not with Rob after the first few months. Now her parents were in South America, and she wasn't about to contact them. No, they were better off not knowing any of this, better off lost in their own lives, and it would make it simpler for her when she moved on after she was discharged from the hospital.

She swallowed cautiously, the pain in her throat easing just a bit. "When *can* I leave?"

"I don't know. I don't have any say in what you do or where you go."

"Then I . . . I need to talk to someone who does," she said.

"I'll see what I can do," R.J. said. He turned, and Lyndsey heard his footsteps on the tile, then the soft whooshing sound of the door closing behind him.

For a second she felt terrified without the cushioning of the man's presence or the sound of his voice, then she closed her eyes and made herself think as clearly as possible. She needed to get her glasses, then she had to make a phone call.

R.J. strode out of the room, nodded to the uniformed policeman sitting on a chair by Lyndsey's door and looked down the hall. He spotted Lyndsey's doctor at the nurses' station and Russ talking on one of the pay phones by the elevators. Quickly he headed for the doctor, a tall, lean man in hospital whites, and told him that Lyndsey had regained consciousness. When the doctor headed down the hall to check on Lyndsey, R.J. walked over to where Russ stood.

As he got near, Russ looked up, said something into the receiver he had pressed to his ear, then hung up. "Is she awake?" he asked immediately.

"Yes. She came out of it a few minutes ago."

"Is she lucid?"

"Scared, but she's making sense."

"That's all I ask," Russ muttered. "Let's go talk to her."

"The doctor's in there right now."

"I'll give him five minutes, then I'm going in to finally get answers."

"There aren't any answers."

"What are you talking about?"

"She says she doesn't remember a thing, that she has no memory of the incident after she got out of her car. She felt someone grab her, then it's a blank."

Russ stared at R.J. hard, then exhaled in a rush. "Is there a punch line to this story?"

"No, that's it."

"What's going on?"

"It could be anything. She might have a form of amnesia specifically manifested by patch memory loss."

"Give that to me in simple English."

"A case of protective forgetfulness, forgetting a segment of the past. Maybe it's a way of dealing with a horror that can't be remembered without pain."

"Any other options?"

"She could be lying, figuring if she doesn't remember anything, she's home free. The killer won't come after her, and we'll let her disappear into the sunset. Or she could be in denial, or she could be in shock. It's a toss-up right now."

"What's your best guess?"

"I can't make one. I know she's scared as hell and wants out of here right now. She sent me to get someone who could get her out tonight."

Russ raked his fingers through his hair and muttered a low curse, then, "God, what a mess. What do we do now?"

"That's up to you. I've got a convention in Chicago that's been going for a day."

Russ pinned R.J. with his dark eyes. "You're walking away from this?"

"I told you I'd be here when she woke up and I'd talk to her. I did. She doesn't remember anything or isn't talking." It wasn't easy saying this, but he knew he had to, especially after his reactions to Lyndsey moments ago. He had to leave, and he knew in his gut that if he went back into that room, if Lyndsey looked at him with those blue eyes, he wouldn't be able to leave. "Bottom line—she's awake, and she's not a witness of any value to you right now."

Russ held up one hand. "Just a minute. That's it? There's nothing else that can be done?"

"Such as?"

"What about drugs or hypnosis to jog her memory or to call her bluff if she's lying?"

R.J. shrugged. "I guess it could be possible, but you're playing with fire. If she's blocked it, remembering it could destroy her. If she's lying, nothing you do will make any difference."

"I don't have a choice, and neither does that woman. We have to do anything it takes to get her to remember or to tell us the truth. What do you think it would take to get her past her amnesia?"

"Time."

"We don't have time. What else is there?"

"Just what you said, hypnosis or drugs. Take your pick. But she has to agree to anything you do."

"Of course, of course. What would it take for her to tell the truth if she's lying?"

"Trusting someone enough to do it."

"Her family—"

He cut off Russ's words. "There isn't any." Saying the words reminded him of what he'd felt when Lyndsey had told him she had no one. "She doesn't have anyone."

Russ rocked forward on the balls of his feet, coming closer to R.J. as he spoke. "Then we need to give her someone she can trust. Someone who instills confidence." He tapped R.J. on the shoulder. "Someone I trust completely."

R.J. shook his head. "I told you I'm done here. I've got a lecture tomorrow."

"Then stay until tomorrow morning. I'm just asking for a bit more time. Come on back in there and we'll do a good guy-bad guy routine."

The lecture was the last thing on his mind. He just wanted out of here and away from an idea that left a bad taste in his mouth. "Count me out."

"All right. That's your choice, but before you go, I need some information."

"What information?"

"How precarious is her mental state?"

"In what way?"

"If push comes to shove, how rough can it get before she'll go over the edge?"

R.J. had never seen this side of his brother-in-law, and it made him sick. Coming so close to Russ that there was less than a foot separating them, he spoke in a low, tight voice. "Listen to me, Russ, and listen well. I know how important it is to get this killer, but I'll be damned if I'll watch you destroy someone else in the process, someone who's only crime was being in the wrong place at the wrong time.''

Russ didn't blink as he muttered, ''I have no intention of destroying anyone except the creep who's running free out there. I just wanted you to know that I might have to do or say things that seem rough.'' He paused, then added, ''But if you'll go back in there with me, you can buffer in case I go too far.''

R.J. almost hated Russ at that moment. He didn't want to be put in the position of rescuing Lyndsey from anyone, or being her shield against the attacks that seemed to be coming at her from all sides. ''I won't play games with her. That's out.''

''This isn't a game, R.J., it's life and death. All you have to do is do what you've done so many times, be there for the victim. That's all.''

He made it sound so simple, but he managed to conjure up the image of Lyndsey when he'd touched her, her hands drawn to her breasts, the pain and confusion in her eyes. He knew that if he didn't go back in there with Russ, someone would, someone who could play the game of good guy-bad guy, someone who would manipulate Lyndsey until the truth came out. He couldn't let that happen. He couldn't just walk away, not yet. ''All right, I'll go back in there with you, but I can't promise that anything I do will work.''

''Let's get in there and find out what's going on.''

Before R.J. could say anything else, Russ turned and headed back to Lyndsey's room. Before they got to the door, Dr. Levin came out and started toward them.

''How's she doing?'' Russ asked as the three men met about ten feet from the door to Lyndsey's room.

"Remarkably well for what she's been through," the balding man said. "But she won't take any medication. I'm ordering something for the pain, and if you can get her to take it, she's going to feel a lot better." He glanced at his watch. "I'll be back in a few hours. If you need anything before then, have me paged."

"Thanks," Russ murmured, then turned and headed for Lyndsey's room. R.J. nodded to the doctor, then followed Russ. As the door closed, R.J. crossed to stand at the foot of the bed and look down at Lyndsey.

She was very still with her eyes closed, the IV gone and the monitor off. As he looked at her paleness and obvious vulnerability, he knew he hadn't had a choice back there with Russ. There was no way he could have left. He'd been fooling himself all along. He wasn't leaving at all. He'd do whatever it took to help her through this and let her get on with her life. That admission bothered him a lot, but not as much as the idea of her being victimized another time.

Russ was at the side of the bed, and when he said her name, she stirred. Her lashes fluttered, then she opened her eyes, the blueness as much a shock to R.J. as it had been the first time.

Lyndsey heard someone say her name, and she slowly opened her eyes. She was aware of a blurred image to her right, a man who said her name again. But it wasn't R.J. talking, and she couldn't begin to understand the degree of disappointment in her that he hadn't come back. She exhaled, feeling tightness in her ribs, and rawness as the air passed through the inside of her mouth.

"I'm Detective MacClain," the stranger said. "The doctor says that you're doing very well. Do you feel up to talking to me for a few minutes?"

She touched her tongue to her tender lips, then managed to say in a hoarse whisper, "Water . . . please."

The shadows shifted, then she felt the straw at her mouth, but this time she could draw the cool liquid onto her tongue with a degree of ease. Then she sank back, letting the water rest in her mouth before she slowly let it slide down her throat. Her muscles contracted painfully for an instant, then eased, and the coolness wandered down toward the aching in her middle.

"Do you need more?" the detective asked.

"No." Her voice still sounded strange to her, but it was a bit stronger when she spoke again. "But, I . . . I need my glasses. I had them—"

"We found a pair by your car," he said. "I brought them with me just in case you needed them." His image moved, then he was saying, "Here, let me help you." She closed her eyes as he carefully eased the cool plastic over her ears, then the weight of the frames and lenses settled on her nose.

She exhaled before slowly opening her eyes to a clear, focused world. And the first image she saw clearly was a man at the foot of the bed.

Dark hair streaked with gray and long enough to rest on the nape of his neck was carelessly swept back from an angular face dominated by a strong jaw and hooded eyes shadowed by dark brows. He looked tall and whipcord lean—all sharp lines and angles—and was dressed in a tweed jacket over a black turtleneck shirt.

"Do you feel up to talking to Russ?" he asked, and she knew the voice. And as she tried to absorb her relief that R.J. had come back, she realized his looks fit his voice, but not the image she had of cops, at least not any of the police officers she'd dealt with.

"You . . . you're a policeman?" she asked.

The detective spoke before R.J. could. "No, he's a doctor, a psychiatrist."

A doctor. No wonder just his presence was soothing. She glanced to her right at a mountain of a man with irregular features and deep brown eyes under heavy brows. Now, he looked more like her idea of a cop, with a nose that had been broken one too many times, and wearing an ill-fitting suit that looked as if he'd slept in it.

"I'm the cop, and I'm very glad you're finally awake." He smiled, and Lyndsey thought he might look like a cop, but he didn't have that way of making you feel distanced from him. His next words only reinforced that idea. "We're going to be seeing a lot of each other, and I want to make this as easy as I can for you. First, can I call you Lyndsey?"

"Yes."

"I'm Russ." He took a breath, and the smile faded with each word he said next. "We don't have the luxury of unlimited time on our hands, so I'll get right down to the basics. I talked to R.J. outside, and he says you claim you don't remember what happened to you."

The illusion fled with the use of the word "claim," and she recognized that tone cops use that tells you they don't believe you, but they aren't going to call you a liar. "I don't remember anything. I just want to get out of here."

Russ shook his head. "Not just yet."

She looked down at her hands and saw bruises at her wrists. Hesitantly she touched the pale blue-and-purple marks circling her right wrist.

"That's from the cord he used to tie you up," Russ said bluntly.

She stared at it, and that familiar feeling of having no control came back in a flood. She covered her right wrist with her left hand and looked away to meet R.J.'s gaze. "I have to leave. You said you'd help."

Before R.J. could say anything, Russ spoke up and drew her full attention. "Lyndsey, you've got bruises and pain, but the other women are dead. We need your help, and you need to heal. So you'll stay here in protective custody and make things easier for all of us."

He gripped the side rail, and intensity was evident in every line of his body. "Let's be frank. We have a killer out there, a killer who's going to strike again and again, and you're the only one who's seen him and lived. And you're an artist, you can give us a description of his face."

"I'm a graphic artist, not a portrait artist," she said flatly.

"But his face is in your mind."

"And I don't remember."

"I know what you said. But when it gets out that you've regained consciousness, the killer is going to think you can finger him."

"But I can't," she said. "You know I can't. Tell the press I can't."

"I could do that, but do you think he'd believe that you developed amnesia? What would you do if you were a killer and knew one person could destroy you completely?"

He was right. No matter if it was Rob after her or this killer, he wouldn't believe that she couldn't remember. "That's why I have to...to go," she said hoarsely.

"Go where? You aren't in any condition to walk out of here, and you have nowhere to go. After you tell us everything, we'll give you around-the-clock protection."

This was all wrong, all crazy. "I...I just have to go...to..."

Russ broke in. "You're here until I say you can go."

"You can't—"

"Yes, I can," he said tightly.

Then help came swiftly as R.J. moved around to the other side of the bed and faced Russ. "She's not the criminal, Russ."

The big man looked at R.J. "She is if she walks away from this. I won't let her."

"Back off. She's the victim, the way the whole city is."

"Yeah, and there'll be more victims if she walks, R.J. I won't let her do that."

"She's not under arrest."

"She should be."

"You're way out of line. She's been through hell, and you're just making things worse."

"How much worse can it get, R.J.?"

R.J. looked down at Lyndsey, and Lyndsey could have sworn she saw a look flash in his eyes, a look that said, "You're not alone in this." Then it was gone, and R.J. turned back to Russ. "She could be dead."

As the sound of his words hung in the air between the two men, Lyndsey experienced something that scared her almost as much as the horror she'd awakened to earlier. She wanted to believe what she saw in R.J.'s eyes, to tell him everything about Rob and let him take care of it. But she stopped herself and retreated from the idea. No matter what she imagined she saw, she was in this alone.

Russ was right in one way. She was too weak to leave under her own power. Pervasive weakness robbed her of the ability to do anything more than lie in bed. She needed whatever protection she could get until she was stronger—until she knew if Rob or a faceless killer was after her. If she stayed for a day or so and let them talk to her, maybe she'd remember, and she'd know the face of her attacker. She touched her tongue to her bruised lips and knew how simple it all was. If they could use her, she could use them until she could get away. "You . . . you won't give out my name, will you?" she asked in a shaky voice.

"No," Russ said. "We'll leave it that you're unidentified and in a coma."

"And you'll give me protection?"

"Around the clock," Russ said quickly.

"No one can get in here?"

"Only me, R.J. and the selected medical staff."

"All right. I'll stay."

"Thanks," Russ said, then motioned to R.J. with one hand. "And the good doctor's going to do what he can to help you remember."

She looked at R.J., and shock rocketed through her. He was smiling at her, a slow, easy smile with none of the seriousness and tension that had been there moments ago. The change in the man's face was staggering, taking years off his age and putting a warm gleam in his eyes. It made Lyndsey's chest tighten.

"I've got the room right next door, so I can be here on a moment's notice if you need me. We'll work this out." He moved, his hand touching the railing, and Lyndsey was inordinately aware of the strong fingers closing over the metal. "Trust me," he said.

The idea that had come to her just moments ago came back full force. If only she could trust him. Then nausea nudged at her. Hadn't she learned? Hadn't she found out the hard way that she couldn't trust or count on anyone? She closed her eyes to shut out the sight of R.J. with his green eyes and gentle smile, and everything came into perspective. A soft voice and touching smile could hide a monster—a monster that could leap out at any moment and destroy her. No, she would trust herself, and she knew what she had to do. She had to call Dallas.

Opening her eyes, she shifted her head to the right and saw the telephone not more than a foot from the bed on the side table. "I...I'm so tired. I need to rest for a bit."

"We need to talk," Russ said quickly.

"She can't tell you anything just yet," R.J. intervened. "Why not give her a few hours to rest, then we'll see what we can do?"

"All right. A few more hours won't hurt, I guess," he said begrudgingly as he looked at his watch. "It's almost midnight. I'll be back around two o'clock."

"Could you put down the side rails before you go?" she asked without opening her eyes.

She heard the metal slide on both sides, then R.J. said, "Do you want me to put your glasses away for you?"

"No," she said quickly, almost afraid to be plunged into that blurred, unfocused world again. "I...I can do it," she said.

"The doctor left a prescription for pain pills. You probably should take them."

Drugs. The idea scared her. What she needed was to get more control, not lose what little control she had. "No, I don't want them."

"Okay. I'll be right next door or in the hospital. If there's any problem, or if you need to talk, just ring for the nurse. She'll find me."

"All right," she said, then concentrated on breathing slowly and evenly, ignoring the rawness in her throat. She heard the two men walking away, the door whooshing open, then shut. Finally silence filled the room.

More weary than she ever remembered being, she lay still with her eyes closed, and it was so tempting to let herself drift, to swing into the forgetfulness of sleep. But she stopped herself. She could sleep later, after she knew where Rob was.

Making herself open her eyes, she lifted her right hand and tried to reach the telephone on the side table. But the instrument was beyond her reach by six inches, and when she tried to shift to get closer, she knew she couldn't do it. There was no strength in her to move anymore. She drew her hand back to rest on her stomach, and she closed her eyes.

She'd rest for a while, then try again to make the call. She had to find out if Rob was in Dallas. If he was, she'd be more certain of what to do here. If he wasn't, she knew where he was. Ever so slowly she felt herself sinking into the softness of natural sleep, and with nothing left in her to fight it, she gave in and let go.

R.J. waited until they were halfway between the elevator and the closed door of Lyndsey's room before he spoke in a low, harsh voice to Russ. "What you did in there stunk."

Russ kept walking, nodded to the officer who was on duty by the elevators, then stopped in front of the closed doors. He pushed his hands in his pockets and cast R.J. a tense look. "I told you I'd do what I had to. And she's agreed to stay."

R.J. looked at the uniformed officer, a rookie named Donaldson, and when they made eye contact, the younger man nodded and knew enough to move back down the hall, putting a discreet distance between himself and the two men. R.J. looked back at Russ. "Why didn't you just pull your gun and hold it to her head? It would have been more direct and more honest.''

Russ pushed the down button for the elevator, then said something that R.J. wasn't prepared for. "What I did worked just fine. She's starting to trust you, R.J. I saw the way she looked at you.''

R.J. remembered that moment of eye contact with Lyndsey, when she'd first looked at him with her glasses on, and the way the lenses had made her eyes seem even larger and more vulnerable. Then when Russ had been badgering her, when she'd looked to him and he'd seen such pain in the blue depths of her gaze, he'd found himself facing off with Russ as if they were enemies. Right now he felt as if this man by him was a stranger, more of a stranger to him than the woman in the room down the hall. "Can't you tell she's scared spitless?''

"And she's got our answers in her head,'' Russ said.

R.J. grabbed Russ's arm as the elevator doors slid open. He wasn't going to let him get away with this. "I told you about games before we went in there.''

Russ looked down at R.J.'s hand on his arm, then shrugged out of the grasp. "I told you I'll do whatever it takes to get this creep.'' He stepped on the elevator and reached to hold the door open with one hand as he looked out at R.J. Then he motioned with his head to the empty elevator car behind him. "I'm going down to get coffee. Are you coming?''

"No.'' R.J. didn't trust himself to get in a closed area with Russ right now. He felt such pure anger that it would be impossible to sit across the table from Russ and drink coffee as if everything was all right. "I've got things to do in my room, and I promised Lyndsey I'd be close by if she needed me.''

"You're really on this case now, aren't you?''

"What do you mean?"

"You're involved, R.J., as in—you'll be there to the end."

"You pulled me into it," he countered.

"So I did," Russ murmured. "You told her you'd be there for her if she needed you."

"That's right."

"How long will you be there for her?"

"Until she remembers."

Russ didn't even look surprised. He just nodded, then dropped his hand and let the elevator doors begin to close. "See you at two," he said.

R.J. watched the doors slide shut and found himself staring at his own reflection in the polished metal doors. Even though his agreement to stay to the end had come grudgingly, he knew that since Lyndsey had opened her eyes and he'd looked into them, the decision had been in place. He had just needed time to recognize that fact.

So he'd be here, and he'd stop Russ from doing whatever it took to get the killer. He glanced back at Lyndsey's closed door. R.J. wouldn't be a party to anything if it meant hurting Lyndsey Cole more than she had already been hurt. His stomach churned at that idea.

He tried to sort through his reactions, the myriad of ups and downs he'd felt since agreeing to come here. He couldn't label most of them, but one he clearly recognized was an incredible protectiveness for a woman he'd just met.

R.J. turned and walked past the young policeman. He needed rest and time to think in quiet. He headed for his room. In the morning he'd call the conference coordinators and tell them he had an emergency and wouldn't be there at all.

He slowed as he passed Lyndsey's door, told the officer on duty there that he'd be in his room if he was needed, then kept walking. Russ was right. He was in this up to his neck, but it wasn't quite as unsettling as it sounded when Russ had said it. The basic need to help, which drew him into the field of psychiatry, was still there, a need Maddy used to call his "take in the strays" weakness.

He stopped at the door to his room, prepared for any feeling at the memory of Maddy—except for the one that came. This was the first time in three years that he didn't feel pain and emptiness, just sadness for what was gone and the remarkable impulse to smile at the humor in the memory.

Stages of grief. He'd told others about them so often, yet he'd forgotten they existed until now. He pushed back the door and walked into the darkened room. He started across to the windows, then almost went to the right, to the connecting door between his room and Lyndsey's. But he stopped himself and went to the bed instead. He slipped off his jacket, laid it across the back of a wooden chair to one side, then took the suitcase he'd originally packed for Chicago off the bed and put it on the floor.

Without undressing, he lay down on the bed and stretched out on the firm mattress. He rested his forearm over his eyes and tried to relax, but he found that difficult. No matter how he tried, his mind wouldn't stop sorting through what had happened tonight, and all those thoughts centered on the woman next door.

Chapter 4

Rage filled the lone man as he moved across the lobby toward the elevators. He never made eye contact with the hospital personnel or with any of the news people who were camping out in the dull beige-and-brown space. He walked with a sure, quick stride, acting as if he belonged. And no one even looked at him.

What a mess he'd made of things. He was sure she'd been dead, and he'd never thought of checking before he dumped her in the field. Now she was in a coma, and if that coma ended, she'd be able to tell them everything. He stopped by the elevator doors and jabbed the up button. He knew he had to make very sure she never came out of the coma.

The doors opened, and he stepped into the empty car, then turned and pressed the button for the tenth floor. Only when the door was closed did he allow his hands to clench into tight fists, welcoming the pain of his nails digging into his palms. It kept him focused and in control.

When there was a soft chime and the car stopped, he saw the number for the fifth floor light up. He made his hands relax as the doors opened and a harried-looking orderly stepped in. He nodded to the man in white, got a curt acknowledgement, then the abrupt request, "Push six."

"Sure thing," he said and pushed the floor button. As the car began to move upward, he stared at his own distorted reflection in the brushed metal doors. No one here knew who he was. Certainly not this man who was not more than two feet from him. All the orderly saw was a maintenance man, someone even lower than him in the power structure of the hospital staff.

When the elevator stopped, the doors opened and the orderly hurried off. The man allowed a smile to tug at the corners of his mouth.

No one knew what he looked like. And no one would. The only witness wouldn't live long enough to tell anyone what she knew. As the elevator started upward again, he pushed his hand in his pocket and felt the coil of nylon cord. No, she wouldn't tell anyone anything, and as the elevator stopped, he knew that with any luck this would all be over with tonight.

Lyndsey drifted comfortably for what seemed forever in soft grayness, then, without warning, she was plunged directly into a dream filled with terror. She was back in Dallas, in the house where she'd lived with Rob, standing in the center of the bedroom. Everything looked the same, as if she'd never left, then she heard Rob yelling for her to come to him. His voice echoed through the house, and she looked frantically around for an escape, but as she watched, the room faded and she was in the parking garage in Seattle.

The empty, cavernous area was cold and dimly lit, with heavy shadows on all sides. From somewhere behind her, she heard Rob coming for her, his footsteps striking the floor and echoing through the space. She could feel the air move with each step he took, stirring soul-deep coldness, and she caught his scent.

She wanted to run, to take off and never look back, but she couldn't move. She wanted to scream, but her throat was tight and no sounds would come. Then she saw someone coming out of the darkness ahead, a man, R.J. He silently approached her, his hands extended toward her, and she knew he'd come to help her and protect her. All she had to do was reach out to him. But no matter how hard she tried to lift her hands, she couldn't. They felt as if they had bracelets of lead on them.

"Come to me," he said softly. "Trust me."

And she wanted to feel his touch, to have him hold her and shield her, and she fought to raise her hands. She looked into his eyes, feeling him urging her on, giving her strength, and she felt her hands begin to lift. But before she could make the connection with him, she felt Rob grabbing her painfully by her upper arm and jerking her away from R.J., and she knew she was lost.

"I'll kill you," Rob was screaming as he spun her around. "I'll kill you and no one will ever know."

She felt her world explode, the rage in her like a fire, and she lifted her hand to strike out. But as she turned and looked at the man who had her by the arm, she realized he had no face.

R.J. heard Lyndsey scream, and he was off the bed and running through the darkened room for the con-

necting door before he had time to think. He pulled open
the door and ran into the dimly lit room. At the same
moment, the policeman who had been outside the door
broke in from the hallway, his gun drawn.

R.J. spun to his left and saw Lyndsey in the middle of
mussed sheets, on her knees in the flimsy hospital gown,
her arms flailing wildly as if fending off blows, and her
eyes wide with raw fear, eyes that were still seeing things
that R.J. knew had been in her dreams. He moved immediately, going to her, destroying the distance between
her and himself in less than a heartbeat. While the policeman snapped on the harsh overhead lights and
searched the room, R.J. reached out to Lyndsey.

But her flailing hands struck him sharply on the arm
as she screamed, "No! Let me go."

R.J. watched helplessly as she scrambled back until
she was pressed against the headboard. Her lips trembled, and he could hear each ragged breath she took.
"Please, please." Her voice faded to a sob, and she
waved her hand weakly through the air as if it was all too
much for her to bear. "Just . . . just let me go."

"What's going on?" the cop asked from behind R.J.

R.J. spoke without looking away from Lyndsey. "A
nightmare," he said. "I'll take care of it. Turn the light
off on your way out and get the doctor in here."

"Sure, I'll get him right away," the cop said, and an
instant later, the lights were out, leaving only the side
light to ward off the darkness.

R.J. could literally see Lyndsey coming back to reality from the horror she'd been lost in. Her eyes began to
focus, her hands fell to her thighs, and she touched her
tongue to her lips. He looked away, saw her glasses on
the floor and dropped to his haunches to pick them up.
He stood and put the glasses on the side table, then care-

fully sat down on the side of the bed. "Lyndsey?" He said her name softly.

She didn't move at first, then she slowly turned her gaze on R.J. Her eyes were shadowed, yet the weak light caught at the unnatural brightness of unshed tears. Despite the ordeal she'd been through, she hadn't cried. She should be crying, yet she wasn't. She wasn't letting herself cry.

"I...I..." she stammered.

Slowly he held up one hand, palm out toward her. "I'm going to touch you, Lyndsey."

When she didn't move or say anything, he shifted, leaning partly on his knees to get closer to her. When he was less than two feet from her, he reached out and touched her hand, which was still curled into a fist. She flinched at the contact, but didn't pull away.

"Lyndsey," he said, almost at eye level with her and so close he could inhale her delicate fragrance. Each breath she took seemed to echo through him. "Tell me what just happened?"

She shook her head slowly, her lips worked, then her eyes fluttered shut and she slowly collapsed, as if whatever had been holding her up had been taken away. She fell forward toward R.J., and he reached out, catching her upper arms. Then he drew her to his chest, folding his arms around her slight form, horribly uncomfortable in a half-sitting, half-on-his-knees position, but he didn't move. He cradled her to him, taking in how small and delicate she felt against him, as insubstantial as the wind that tickles the leaves in summer.

And he felt as if he were slipping back in time to the moments when he had been the comforter instead of the one in desperate need of comforting. He closed his eyes tightly, feeling her shudder with each breath she took, and he gave her what support he could, stroking her hair gently, smoothing the silky cap and whispering in a low voice, "It's all right. It's going to be all right. You're not alone."

Like a wounded animal seeking cover, she snuggled closer, her cheek pressed to the hollow of his shoulder, and she sighed. The sound made her breasts tremble against his chest, and in that moment, everything shifted. His feelings went from something he under-stood and controlled—the comforting and support—to something he didn't understand at first. Then he be-came aware of how neatly she fit into the angles of his body. The hospital gown was borderline indecent in its ability to cover her soft curves or contain her body heat. And as he inhaled her scent, softness mingled with warmth, he felt his own temperature begin to rise. He knew exactly what was going on.

His hands stilled, and he swallowed hard, his eyes closed so tightly he saw explosions of color behind his lids. This was wrong.

He had been so sure there wasn't anything left in him to respond to a woman like this, yet it hadn't changed the fact that every atom of his body was responding, not as a comforter, but as a man. With great determination, he concentrated on what he was supposed to be doing, and on his own professional ethics.

Yet his body didn't understand about oaths and promises. It kept responding, the need in him to do more than hold Lyndsey and comfort her growing at an un-settling rate until he was fighting wild fantasies that only increased his discomfort. Before, he'd wondered if she was loved, but now he wondered what it would be like to make love with her.

He forced himself to stop those thoughts, telling himself he was alone, that the intensity of the moment was distorting everything. It couldn't be anything else. He wouldn't let it be. Lyndsey Cole was a patient, a woman he wanted to help...whom he needed to help. And he cared on that level. But he wouldn't violate every ethical promise he'd ever made himself.

More important than anything professional, he'd made a personal law for himself. He'd never care too much about any woman again. It hurt too much to lose a part of himself. And he was sure he wouldn't survive a second loss.

With a great effort of will, he gently took Lyndsey by her shoulders and held her away from him. When he looked into her huge, shadowy eyes, it was all he could do not to draw her back. He dropped his hands and slipped off the bed. Distance. He needed as much physical distance from Lyndsey as he could get without leaving the room.

Lyndsey had weakly fallen into R.J.'s heat and strength, and for a few minutes she had felt comforted and protected and safe, things she had never felt before in her life. She had needed that desperately after the dream, and she'd allowed herself to lean against R.J., to close her eyes and let him support her.

But even as he'd stroked her hair and told her everything would be all right, she had known the magnitude of that lie. As great a lie as her believing that she could trust anyone to protect her and keep her safe. She'd thought, for a brief time, that Rob could, but she'd been wrong, almost dead wrong. And she'd known how wrong she could be again. No, it had all been a delusion, something bred of fear and a dream about a man who could be an anchor...and a faceless man who wanted to kill her.

She stiffened with memory at the same time R.J. shifted, drawing back and holding her by her shoulders. She looked at him and saw only a blur. It was easier that way, and she was almost thankful he'd pulled away. This was business for him, to comfort emotionally unstable people. R.J. let her go and got off the bed, and she ignored the sudden feeling of isolation and reached for the sheet that was tangled around her.

Awkwardly she tugged at the fabric until she could push her legs under it, then she sank back in the bed. R.J. was silently watching her, and she blocked him out while she pulled the sheet up to her middle, then she rested her forearm protectively over her eyes. She tried to take even breaths in hopes of easing the tension in her, but no easing came. The tension only increased while the dream and her reactions to R.J. stayed so treacherously fresh in her mind.

The door opened, and someone came into the room. When he spoke, she recognized Dr. Levin's voice. "The officer told me you need me in here."

"There's been a bit of an emotional upheaval," she heard R.J. say, his voice farther from the bed now. "A nightmare."

Lyndsey lowered her arm, letting it rest across her middle, and she glanced to her right, but the world was a blur of shapes and shadows again. For a moment, she thought of letting it stay that way, then she knew not being able to see didn't change what was out there.

"I thought you were doing so well when I saw you last," the doctor said from close by.

"I'm all right," she replied in a voice that was annoyingly unsteady. "But, my glasses, they fell off."

"They're on the table," she heard R.J. say, but it was the doctor who handed them to her.

She took them from him and slipped them on, blinking a couple of times to focus on the dimly lit room, then she glanced at the doctor. "Thanks."

"Now," he said as he lifted her wrist and checked her pulse, "how do you feel?"

She exhaled, and it was then the pain came back, or maybe she just hadn't been aware of it until now. But when she swallowed, the rawness seemed to be even worse and her ribs ached. "Everything hurts, my throat, my chest, my arms and legs."

"I told you earlier, you really should consider taking something for the pain. It'll make it easier for you to rest and regain your strength if you can relax a bit."

"I don't want anything," she said, afraid to be drugged, knowing that she had to be conscious and aware of everything. "I won't take anything that knocks me out."

"I understand. I can give you a shot that will lessen the pain and let you relax. You won't sleep unless you want to sleep. It'll make you feel as if you've had a couple of drinks." He let go of her wrist, and she drew her hand back to rest it on her stomach. "You need it. Your heart's pounding like a drum."

She knew her increased heart rate was from the dream, but also from what had happened with R.J. She could see him in her peripheral vision somewhere to her right, but she kept her gaze on the doctor. The idea of going for even a short time without pain was very appealing. Maybe just once, just for a while. "All right," she finally agreed. "But not anything too strong."

"Very mild," the doctor assured her, then reached for her arm and pressed the softness at the inside of her el-

bow with his thumb several times. Then he turned, took
a hypodermic from a nurse Lyndsey hadn't even noticed was in the room, and murmured, "This'll only hurt
for a moment."

As he primed the needle, Lyndsey looked away and
her gaze touched R.J. standing by the connecting door.
Their eyes made contact, and the intensity of his expression made her chest tighten. Quickly she looked
away, and as the needle pressed to her skin, she closed
her eyes. Then she felt the sting of the injection and she
grimaced.

When she opened her eyes, she didn't look at R.J., but
at the doctor. Heat spread up her arm. "There," Dr.
Levin said as he drew back. "It should work fairly
quickly." He looked over his shoulder at R.J. "I'll be on
call all night. If you need anything, just have them get
me." He looked down at Lyndsey again. "You can ring
the buzzer," he said, then with a soft pat on her arm, he
turned and left with the nurse.

As Lyndsey watched the door close, R.J. came toward the bed, reached for a chair by the table, drew it to
the bedside and sat down. Lyndsey closed her eyes and
settled back in the pillows, already feeling a certain
softness coming over her. And the pain began to ebb.

Yet even with her eyes closed and the drug beginning
to work, she was totally aware of R.J. Then he spoke
through the stillness, his deep voice edged by a velvety
roughness. "Are you all right now?"

The possibility of her being "all right" was so remote
at that moment that she almost laughed. But there was
no humor in her, even for the absurd. "Yes," she lied on
a soft whisper. "Fine."

"Do you want me to leave?"

She had felt good about finally being alone until Friday night. Now the idea of being alone in the darkness held real fear for her. "No," she said before she could stop the word, then she opened her eyes and stared at the shadows over her. The pain was being pushed to a place where it was almost unable to touch her, yet she didn't feel drugged or fuzzy at all. "I...I don't want to be alone right now," she found herself admitting.

"Would it hurt you to talk a bit?"

She swallowed, feeling tightness in her throat, but none of the raw pain. "No, I don't think so."

"Do you want to talk about the dream?"

The dream? No, she didn't want to relive it, and she certainly didn't want to tell him he was in the dream, that he'd seemed to be her savior, then had turned out to be as helpless as she had been in the wake of Rob's anger and rage. "No, I...don't."

"What would you like to talk about?"

You, she thought, the idea coming without warning. How you make me feel things I never have before, things I would have died for before. And it's all your job, something you offer to all your patients. But she said none of those words out loud. Instead, she let the gentleness of the drug surround her, and the relaxation in her body was so welcome she almost smiled. Like two drinks? Yes, that's exactly how she felt.

Then she heard herself asking something she couldn't even remember thinking about before that moment. "What's your real name?"

She heard the chair shift on the tile as R.J. settled. "I told you before. R. J. Tyler."

"R.J.?"

"That's it."

"That's what?"

He chuckled softly, an unexpected but soothing sound. "My name."

"Is your real name so bad you have to use initials?"

"That all depends what your definition of bad is."

She turned slightly so she could see his shadow not more than three feet from the bed, and a name came from her childhood. "My definition of bad is Rooney Jubert."

That brought a full burst of rough laughter from R.J., and the sound seemed to seep into Lyndsey's soul. "That's a real name?" he asked.

"A long time ago, I knew someone named that. But I think that was his full name, his first and last, not his first and his middle."

"Well, I'm not a Rooney Jubert."

She looked away from R.J. to the ceiling again, uncomfortably aware of a growing sense of freedom in her to talk. It had to be the drug. Like two drinks. Her alcohol tolerance was nil, and she got talky after just a couple of drinks. Just like now. "I didn't think you were a Rooney, but you sort of look like a Richard."

"Wrong. What about your name?" he asked.

"My name?"

"How did you get the name Lyndsey?"

The truth came out with relative ease and acceptance, instead of the usual bitterness. "It was the first name my parents heard after I was born. The doctor who delivered me was called Farren Lyndsey. I'm lucky they didn't give me his first name."

"I guess so," he said on a soft chuckle. "That's not your middle name, is it?"

"No, I don't have a middle name." She'd made up her own middle names, soft names like Wendy or Tara. But all she had was a blank space on any forms she filled in.

"My father thought it wasn't necessary. Lyndsey Cole. That's all." She slipped off her glasses and held them in her hand resting on her stomach. She didn't mind the blur and softness now. It fit the way she was feeling. The emotions of moments ago seemed as if they had never been, but she remembered the scene she'd made. "I'm sorry," she murmured.

"Sorry you don't have a middle name?" he asked in a voice touched with humor.

"No, about creating a scene like that and causing so much trouble."

"You were scared, weren't you?"

"Yes," she admitted easily.

"Then you don't need to be sorry. Everyone gets scared. God knows you're entitled to be scared after what you've been through."

He made everything sound so rational. "I guess so."

"What was it that scared you in the dream?"

She closed her eyes and let his voice surround her. "I don't remember," she said, not wanting to examine the terror she felt when she thought of Rob.

"What would you think scares most people in this world?" he said through the shadows.

"Is this a quiz?"

"No, just wondering what you think?"

"Oh, free association?"

"You know the term?"

That sobered her completely. She knew the term. The counselor she'd contacted to help her fix her marriage had used the term. That was about all she remembered from that aborted attempt. "I remember it from somewhere. So, what do you want to do? You say scared, and I say..."

"You'd say what?"

Two days ago, she would have said "no more" or "over with," but not now. "I'd say 'of course'."

"Why?"

"Isn't everyone scared at one time or another?"

"Sure. You've known someone who was afraid, haven't you?"

The person she used to be had lived in that state for so long it had seemed as if it had been forever. "Yes."

"Was it reasonable for that person to be afraid?"

"Yes." She'd been afraid to say the wrong thing, do the wrong thing.

"What was this person afraid of?"

She took a breath, finding the action as easy as the talking was right now, and the answer came before she thought of lying. "When she was little it was fear of being alone. She was always alone. She was in boarding schools all year, even for vacations. Except once, her parents met her in Spain for the summer." She exhaled. "That was nice."

"They loved her, didn't they?"

"Of course they did, in their own way. But her father was a career diplomat, and her mother was a career diplomat's wife. That was her career. They moved around, and it wasn't any sort of life for a child. I often wondered why they even had a child."

"What happened to her?"

"She learned to make do, to be by herself, and she had imaginary friends. That helped. And she went out on her own as soon as she could. She depended on herself."

"And was she afraid all this time?"

"Off and on. Sometimes she felt as if she was being swallowed up by the world, and sometimes she thought she'd found the pot of gold at the end of the rainbow."

R.J. was silent, and Lyndsey kept talking, letting words fall over words, as if saying them in the darkness and in the third person made them safe to say. "But she never did find the pot of gold." She thought of when she'd met Rob and grimaced inside. "She didn't even get close."

"And it scared her?"

"It ended up terrifying her."

"What happened?"

She closed her eyes tightly, fingering her glasses in her hand. "She met this man, a quiet nice man, and she fell in love. He was attentive and kind, and she thought she'd found roots, a connection."

"Didn't she?"

"No, not even close."

"Why?"

She exhaled. "He wasn't the person she thought he was. He...he changed into someone she didn't even know right after they were married."

"How did he change?"

She almost didn't finish, wanting to keep the words inside, but feeling for the first time in a long while that she was safe saying them. "He hurt her. He got angry at the littlest thing, and yelled and screamed at her. He said it was because he was under horrible pressure at work and that she was stupid. And she tried so hard to make things right."

"Did she?"

"No, she couldn't."

"And that scared her?"

Scared wasn't a strong enough word. "She...she was terrified." Her hand tightened on her glasses, and it felt as if she would snap the plastic frame. "She worried about setting him off. Worried about doing the wrong thing, saying the wrong thing, even looking the wrong way. She gave up the idea of having children, and gave up the idea that love was the greatest cure-all in this world.''

"He abused her physically?" R.J. asked bluntly.

She flinched, her pain not physical now, but just as potent as any bruised ribs. "Y-yes, but he actually did her some good."

"In what way?"

"He taught her that she couldn't trust anyone to be who they seemed to be, that she'd been right all along. She could only trust herself."

"And you think that's good?"

"It's the only way to survive."

R.J. was silent for a long while, then he asked, "What happened to her?"

"She put up with it until she couldn't any longer."

"Then what?"

"She disappeared." As each word was uttered, she felt herself getting more and more weary. "Poof, gone, vanished. But..."

"But?"

She turned away from R.J., rolling onto her side and pulling her knees up to her stomach. "He'll find her. He said he would, and he will."

"But if she disappeared completely, how could he find her?"

"I don't know," she murmured. "But he will."

She heard R.J. move, then he spoke again and she could tell he was farther from the bed. "Then what's she going to do?"

"I don't know," she said again, her voice thick with coming sleep. She felt drained, as if she'd run a marathon race, and she gave into the weariness. "I wish I did," she murmured. Then she let go and slipped into sleep. And her last thought was thankfulness that R.J. hadn't left her alone in the night.

Chapter 5

R.J. stared out the window, not daring to move or look back at Lyndsey. He'd been so sure, when he'd let her go after the dream, that he'd managed to put professional distance between himself and her. But he had never been more wrong in his life.

He heard her regular breathing and small muffled sounds as she fell into sleep. Thank goodness she could rest for a while, but he was far from it himself. Agitation churned at his stomach, and a burning anger ate at him.

So that was why she was running, why she had no background, no home base? The man she'd married and trusted to give her the love she'd never felt as a child had abused her. The ring was gone from her finger, but not the memories or the horrors.

The idea that anyone would hurt her was so foreign to R.J. that he had to try and absorb the fact along with the rising outrage that was filling him. It was hard enough to think about this demented killer attacking her, but how in the hell could a man who claimed to love her damage her like this? Wasn't love about protecting, about sheltering, about nurturing?

He raked his fingers through his hair and exhaled on a rush. Damn him for what he'd done to Lyndsey. The depth of his hatred for the man shook R.J.—it wasn't just professional outrage. He knew if her husband walked into this room right now, he'd have a hard time restraining himself from killing him.

That last idea stopped R.J. in his tracks. Anger was one thing, justifiable anger, but this rage was an emotion he had felt so rarely in his life that he couldn't assimilate it. He heard Lyndsey sigh softly as she fell deeper and deeper into sleep.

He turned, and through the dim light, he saw her curled into a semifetal position, a position of self-protection. He felt a literal pain in the region of his heart. As if drawn by a magnet, he went back to the bed and looked down at her. She'd fallen into an easy sleep, with the tension that had been around her mouth and eyes erased for now. Pale hair framed a face with delicate skin and an unguarded expression of vulnerability.

He reached down and took the glasses from her hand, and his fingers brushed her fingers. The heat from her skin shot through him, and he drew back as if he'd been burned. He admitted what he wanted to do was touch her and hold her, but he made himself move away with the glasses. He went around to the other side of the bed and laid the glasses on the side table. Then he sat down in the chair, settled low on the seat with his hands resting on his stomach and exhaled. There wasn't a lot he could do, except be here if Lyndsey woke from a nightmare again. So he'd wait and watch, and take the chance to sort out his own feelings.

The next time Lyndsey woke, she was instantly conscious of everything. She lay very still with her eyes closed, knowing where she was, what had happened, and what she'd let herself say last night. And she knew what she had to do this morning. She opened her eyes to clear sunlight filtering through the partially closed drapes, and she tested her body carefully.

Amazingly the pain was almost gone. She felt stiff and sore, but the real pain had filtered away sometime during the night. And she knew what she had to do. Call Dallas. She was completely alone, so she carefully eased herself up to a sitting position, supporting herself with her hands flat on the bed.

Taking a steadying breath, she swung her legs over the side of the bed. For a moment she was light-headed, then it settled and she reached toward the side table, skimming her fingers over a glass and a small tray before she felt her glasses. She slipped them on, then looked to the table and saw the phone.

Closing her fingers around the cold plastic, she brought the receiver to her ear, then read directions off the base of the phone to get an outside line. When she heard a dial tone, she pressed the numbers for the house in Dallas. After two rings, the answering machine clicked on and she heard Rob's recorded voice. "No one's here right now to take your call. Leave a message, and I'll get back to you when I can."

She put the receiver back, almost sick from the shock of hearing his voice, and sick from the knowledge that he wasn't there at the house. Then she glanced at the clock on the side table. Eight o'clock in the morning.

Ten in Dallas. No wonder he wasn't at the house. He'd be at the office by now.

Carefully she dialed his business number, waited through four rings, then a woman answered. "Sales, Mr. Peters' office. This is Elaine, may I help you?"

"Mr. Peters, please," Lyndsey managed in an only slightly hoarse voice.

"I'm sorry. Mr. Peters isn't available right now, but if you—"

"When *will* he be available?"

"I really don't know. Perhaps Mr. Phillips can—"

"No, I need to talk directly to Mr. Peters. This is an emergency. Just get him on the line."

"I'm sorry," the woman said, her voice tighter now. "That's just not possible."

She took a shaky breath. "All right, tell me when he'll be in his office, and I'll call back then."

"If you call back in a few weeks—"

"A few weeks?"

"Actually he's out of town for a while. But if you would care to—"

Lyndsey hung up on the woman's voice and had to take a deep breath to fight sudden dizziness. A few weeks? God, he *could* be here. It could have been him who had attacked her. Then she had a horrible thought. It had to have been Rob, or why was she the only victim of this killer left alive? Rob had done this to scare her, to let her know she couldn't get away, and he'd be back.

Her first instinct was to find her clothes and run, but she stopped those thoughts. Despite her need to get out of here and disappear again, she wasn't going to do anything without thinking it through, without planning. She'd found that out the hard way the first time she'd left Rob and he'd found her within hours. He'd even found the shelter eventually when she'd left him the last time.

No, the police were here now, and for a while, they would keep everyone away because they thought the killer had done this to her. By the time she knew for sure about Rob, she'd have had a chance to make a new plan and disappear. This time she'd do it right. She wouldn't keep any contacts with her old life, or with this one. Not even with Estelle at the shelter.

Her painfully empty stomach began to churn with sickness, and she saw the open door to the bathroom across the room. Slowly she slipped down the side of the bed until her bare feet touched the cold floor, then pressing her hand to her middle, she managed to walk to the bathroom.

Once in the tiny cubicle, she reached for the sides of the sink and waited as the sickness settled. Then she turned on the faucet and cupped the cool water. Touching it to her cheeks, she looked into the mirror over the sink. Her reflection stunned her.

She looked like a stranger, with her pale skin that showed fading bruises at her eyes and cheek and a bandage at her temple. She touched the gauze, then tugged at the tape until the bandage was off and exposed a jagged cut that was closed and healing. She turned from the sight and went back inside her room.

She felt stronger than she thought she'd be, and she didn't go back to the bed. Instead, she crossed to the windows and looked out at the morning city. Far below, Seattle looked deceptively clean, clear and uncluttered. "Lyndsey?"

She hadn't heard the door open, and the sudden sound of R.J. saying her name stunned her for a moment. But it was something more than his voice that made her heart begin to pound against her ribs as she slowly turned and saw him coming across the room toward her.

Looking up at him from a high hospital bed, she hadn't thought him overly tall. But as he came toward her now, she realized he towered a good six inches above her. And his wiry thinness didn't make him seem any the less imposing. Weariness seemed to cut deep lines at either side of his mouth, but his clothes looked fresh, he wore a blue sports coat, pale blue shirt and dark slacks worn with suede shoes. And his eyes, that peculiar shade of hazel, were heavy-lidded, yet intensely focused on her.

He was exhausted, and she was the reason. She knew from the conversation she'd heard between R.J. and the detective that R.J. was supposed to be out of town now. She was the only reason he was still here, sleeping at a hospital, trying to help a woman he probably thought was neurotic and maybe a bit crazy.

Then he held out his hand, and in an instant she was back in the dream, with him coming to save her. But there was no horror behind her, just this man in front of her, and an overwhelming need to go to him, to let him hold her and surround her with the heat and strength she remembered from last night.

"What are you doing up?" he asked as he got within a few feet of her, his hand falling to his side without touching her.

She motioned nervously toward the window. "I was just looking at the city. I was restless."

He cocked his head to one side and narrowed his eyes as he studied her. And the action made her totally aware of the fact she was standing there in the flimsy hospital gown and little else. "Any more nightmares?" he asked.

That made her feel cold, and as she looked into the depths of his hazel eyes, she saw a look she'd seen so many times in others' faces. He pitied her. She hadn't fooled him at all by pretending she'd been talking about a third party last night. And pity was the last thing she wanted from this man.

"No, no more nightmares," she said, standing very still, fighting the urge to run back to bed and pull the sheets up over her head. "I need to..." She touched her tongue to her lips, then plunged on, "I want to apologize for last night."

"I told you you didn't have to be sorry for being scared by the nightmare."

"No, not that. I was apologizing for telling you all those things last night." She looked away from his intense gaze and stared at her bare feet on the green tiles. "I don't know why I did, unless it was the medication the doctor gave me."

"Didn't it help to talk, Lyndsey?"

She looked up at him, his eyes still intent, but the look had shifted from pity to something she couldn't quite recognize. "No...yes, I guess so, but I shouldn't have told you just the same."

"That's my job. I'm paid to listen, and I heard the story of a woman caught in circumstances, a woman who was strong enough to see her mistakes and take control. She got away the only way she could." His eyes darkened. "And I heard the story of a disturbed man who victimized that woman and probably every other person in his life. You got away from him, Lyndsey. You broke the cycle, his cycle with you. That's the bottom line. It wasn't you, it was him."

She closed her eyes for a moment, then shook her head. "I chose him. I thought I was doing the right thing,'' she whispered. "There was something wrong, something I did wrong."

R.J. came even closer. "You made an error in judgment, but you didn't do anything to make your husband the man he is."

She clasped her hands tightly in front of her. "If I'd done—"

He cut her words off by unexpectedly reaching out to her, touching her, his fingers lightly cupping her chin. "No, it was *nothing* you did. He was sick. He needed help, professional help." His voice was low and suddenly unsteady. "God, no man in his right mind would do anything but love a woman like you."

Lyndsey didn't move, stunned by his actions and his words. And by her reactions to the connection between the two of them. It was as if a shell had been torn from her, and she felt something so strong and so pure, that it couldn't be defined. For a crazy instant, she knew the desire to move closer, to touch R.J., to touch his lips with the tips of her fingers, to experience the feeling of those lips on hers.

As her thoughts wandered off in dangerous directions, she literally had to stop herself from swaying toward R.J. In a flash, she understood what she was doing, what she wanted. And she knew just as instantly that she'd never have it. Thankfully, right then, the door opened and Russ strode into the room.

"Good morning, you two," he said.

R.J. didn't look at Russ right away. His gaze dropped to Lyndsey's lips, then he drew his hand back, and he turned away. Lyndsey felt such a loss that it staggered her.

In a daze, she watched Russ pat R.J. on the shoulder, then as he looked past R.J. at her, she realized how weak

her legs were. As she turned to go back to the bed, she
felt R.J. take her arm, his fingers warm and sure,
steadying her. Gently he helped her, and she knew how
easy it would be to keep leaning on him, to let him support her and help her. Then she faced reality. He
couldn't be her anchor at all, no matter what she'd
thought for those brief moments in the dream.

He helped her ease up onto the bed, and when she was
finally sitting on the edge with her feet dangling over the
side, R.J. let her go. She didn't look at him, but as a chill
came over her, she wrapped her arms around herself to
try and trap what heat she could to her body. Then she
looked up at R.J., who was no more than two feet from
her. Without a word, he touched the wound on her temple, his eyes narrowing. "That doesn't look too bad."

"It's healing," she murmured, then moved her head
to avoid the touch and looked at Russ as he came to
stand by R.J. The detective looked as if he hadn't had a
much more restful night than R.J., but she thought he
probably had that perpetually mussed look that some
men seemed to have no matter what clothes they wore.
It didn't help that Russ MacClain seemed to choose
baggy suits in drab colors.

"You're looking a thousand percent better this
morning," the big man said with a smile that didn't quite
touch his eyes.

Physically Lyndsey felt like a different person, with
pain easing and her throat feeling just a bit tight. But
emotionally she felt even more fragmented, especially
since she'd found out Rob wasn't in Dallas. "I do feel
better," she admitted.

"Any luck remembering?"

"I'm sorry, no," she said and could almost feel the
man's disappointment.

"Are you up to a few questions?" he asked, the smile gone, and the intensity back full force.

"Sure," she murmured.

"Russ?" R.J. said. "If you're going to be here for a while, I've got some things I have to take care of. I'll be back as soon as I can get here."

"Then what?" Russ asked as he looked at R.J.

"We'll do whatever we have to do to stop this nightmare," he said and hesitated. "Whatever Lyndsey agrees to do, I'll try it."

Lyndsey stared down at her hands and didn't look up again until she heard R.J. leave. Then she met Russ's gaze. It was easier now that R.J. was gone. "What did you want to ask me?"

He moved to the foot of the bed and reached for something by the footboard, then a motor whirred softly and the back of the bed rose to a forty-five-degree angle. "First, lie back. Be comfortable."

Lyndsey shifted on the bed until she was resting against the raised back, and she pulled the sheets up to her waist. As she smoothed the cool fabric over her, she looked up at Russ, who had come back to stand by the side. "I feel terrible about taking R.J. away from his own practice like this."

"Don't worry. He's got what you'd call a 'flexible schedule' these days."

She touched her tongue to her lips. "It must be hard on his family."

Russ pushed back both sides of his suit coat, exposing his shoulder holster, and he tucked his hands in his pockets. "Actually I'm his family, and it would be hard on me if he wasn't here."

She didn't see any sort of resemblance to R.J. at all. "You're brothers?"

That brought a bark of laughter from the big man and a genuine smile that settled in his dark eyes. "No, not blood relations. He's my brother-in-law."

R. J. Tyler was married. Lyndsey had no idea why that fact hit her so hard, or why it made her insides clench in the most awful manner. She spread her hands on her stomach, but kept looking at the man. "You're his...his wife's brother?"

"That's the way it works," Russ said as he reached for the chair R.J. had used during the night and sank down on the vinyl seat.

"She...she must be very understanding, what with him staying the night and all."

Russ's face sobered as he settled in the chair. For an instant, Lyndsey clearly saw pain in the man's dark eyes, then it was gone as if he had practiced the move until he had it perfected. "Maddy was very understanding, along with being beautiful. That's probably two of the reasons R.J. was so crazy about her."

"Was?" she asked in a low voice, wondering how any woman in her right mind could walk away from a man like R.J.

"She died three years ago." He said the words bluntly and evenly, yet she could sense the man's pain, almost as sharply as she could imagine the horrible loss that R.J. must have endured.

"I'm sorry."

Russ closed his eyes for a long moment, then opened them again and stared at some spot to the left of Lyndsey. "Sometimes it seems like it just happened. Other times, it seems like it's a memory from another life. Then it's easier to deal with the pain."

She knew the feeling. She could still remember the pain Rob inflicted on her, both physically and emotionally, yet in the same moment, she felt as if everything to do with Rob was from another lifetime. "The human mind has strange ways of dealing with life so you can get through it."

"You're right. You can go through hell and come out of it, and it can actually become just an unpleasant memory. It's getting through it that can almost kill you. I didn't think I'd get past Maddy dying."

"Was she in an accident?"

"No, she died suddenly of an aneurysm. She was three years younger than me, my only sister, and I never dreamed I'd outlive her. One minute she was there. She was laughing, so alive, and the next she was gone. She and R.J. were on a vacation, the first they'd taken in years. She was happy. And she was with R.J. I'm thankful for that."

She watched Russ, but all she could think about was what R.J. had gone through. And how he'd survived it. "I guess R.J. dealt with it, I mean, being a psychiatrist and all."

He exhaled harshly. "Physician heal thyself? It doesn't work that way. For the first year, I don't think I saw him sober. The second year, he was like a zombie, only doing what he had to do. Now he's finally back working, but he's so different." He shrugged sharply. "Tragedy changes people."

Lyndsey knew tragedy had changed her, but not a change born out of losing love. It had never been love with Rob. She wasn't even sure she would have recognized love if she faced it head-on.

R.J.'s wife had had love. From the little she knew of R. J. Tyler and what Russ had just told her, she had no doubt his wife had been totally loved. That thought brought such a stabbing sensation to the pit of her stomach she had to press harder there with her hands. R.J. must have loved her completely and totally to grieve so horribly. And for an instant she had the most astounding sense of jealousy. Not directed at R.J.'s wife, but at the fact that she had never known that kind of love, and she never would.

She realized that Russ had been speaking, but she didn't have any idea what he was saying. "I'm sorry?" she asked.

"I said, I'm sure you'll feel different after this is all over. You'll be changed. But at least there's hope here. If you can remember the attack, we can catch this guy."

How could she have totally forgotten why Russ was here? He hadn't come in to tell her about R.J., about his love for his wife, or make her feel more lonely than she had ever felt in her life. "I'll try, but there's still no face in my memory."

"Then we'll work from a different angle. Just tell me again what happened, and don't leave anything out, no matter how small or insignificant you think it is."

Lyndsey closed her eyes and recited the incident as if she was a third party watching from a distance. And for the next half hour, Russ picked at her story, asking questions that she couldn't begin to think had any bearing on the case. "Had you had supper before the attack?" "Where did you eat?" "Exactly how were you touching the car when he grabbed you?" "Do you remember heat or cold?" "Had you worked that day?"

She answered as much as she could and really didn't have to lie. He never asked her again if she thought she knew the attacker. He never asked her again if she was lying. "I just wish I could tell you more," she said.

Russ sat back in the chair, silently writing in a small notebook he had, then he looked up at her. He was about to say something else, but his words were cut off when the door opened. Lyndsey looked toward the door, but it wasn't R.J. A nurse came in carrying a tray. "Dr. Tyler told me you were awake and might want something to eat," she said in a cheerful voice as she came to the bed. "So I went to the cafeteria and picked out a selection for you."

Lyndsey almost refused, then she caught a whiff of toast and realized she hadn't eaten anything by mouth for a day and a half. She looked at Russ. "Is it all right?"

He motioned with one hand. "Sure. Go ahead. We can talk while you eat."

The nurse put the tray on a portable table, then swung the table over Lyndsey's lap and took the cover off the food. "There's a bit of everything. If you need anything else, just ring."

"Thank you," Lyndsey said and looked down at toast, orange juice, cut-up orange slices, a pot of tea and a dish of soft boiled eggs.

As the nurse left, Lyndsey picked up a piece of toast and began to nibble on it, and Russ sank down in the chair. He slouched low and clasped his hands loosely on his middle. "You were married, weren't you?" he asked without warning.

Lyndsey stopped chewing, the food suddenly very dry on her tongue. Reaching for the orange juice, she almost lied to the man, then realized how foolish that would be after the way she had exposed herself to R.J. the night before. "I was," she said before she sipped the cool juice.

"Is he dead?"

She flinched at the idea, remembering the times she'd lain in the dark at the shelter and wished Rob was dead.

"No, he's not," she said, putting the orange juice back and staring at the dish of eggs. "We're divorced."

"Do you want us to contact him about what happened?"

"No," she said quickly. "I mean, he's out of my life now."

"That's too bad," Russ murmured. "Everyone needs someone when they're going through rough times." He narrowed his eyes. "You don't have anyone?"

"No, not really." She broke a piece of toast in two and stared at the two pieces. "My parents are out of the country, and they couldn't do anything about this, anyway."

"What about the dream?"

So, he knew and that's why he didn't come back last night. "It was a nightmare."

"About the attack?"

"Not really." She broke the toast into small pieces and let them drift into the dish with the eggs. "Just blurred images and general confusion."

"The officer who had the night duty said you raised the roof. He was sure someone had gotten to you."

She dropped the mutilated piece of toast and sat back. "Could someone get in here?"

"No, you're covered."

"Detective—"

"Russ, please."

"I can't stay here much longer. I've...I've got things I need to do. I've got my life, and—"

The door opened and Lyndsey looked up, expecting R.J., but it wasn't him this time, either. Instead, a uniformed officer looked inside. "Sir?" he said to Russ. "Donner says he needs to see you right away."

Russ lifted his large frame out of the chair with amazing speed. "Be right back," he said to Lyndsey, then headed for the door.

When he'd gone and the door had swung shut behind him, Lyndsey stared down at her food with a frown, then pushed the table away. She had no idea why she felt so disturbed by what Russ had told her about R.J.'s life. Yet she was.

She sank back in the pillows and with great effort brought her thoughts back where they belonged. What was she going to do about Rob?

"We found this just a few minutes ago," Officer Donner said as he pointed to four tiny balls of foil on the floor just inside the stairwell door about thirty feet past the elevators. "I was checking at the end of the shift and opened the door to make sure it was all clear in the stairwell and spotted them."

Russ stared at the floor, at the balled-up pieces of foil he'd seen before. "No one saw anything?"

"No, sir."

Russ pulled on a thin plastic glove, then dropped to his haunches and nudged at one of the balls with the tip of his finger. "Good work, Donner. These could be important."

"If you hadn't told me about the gum, I wouldn't have thought anything about it." The information that gum wrappers had been found near the crime scenes where the other victims had been abducted hadn't been released to the press or the public. "Did you find them where the Cole woman was attacked?"

Russ stood and shook his head. "No. Are you sure you didn't see anyone out of the ordinary hanging around here?"

"No, sir. Just people who should be here."

"Such as?"

"Our people. The medical staff. Maintenance. A janitor came by to say there'd been some electrical problems on the next floor and wondered if we'd had any problems up here."

"Where was he?"

"On the elevator. He never got off. He'd just left when the woman screamed."

"Russ?" R.J. came up behind the uniformed cop and looked past him at Russ. "What's going on?"

"Don't know just yet," he said, then spoke to Donner. "Get the lab boys up here and tell them to rush whatever they find on the papers."

"Yes, sir," Donner said, then hurried off.

R.J. came into the doorway. "Get the lab boys for what?"

Russ pointed to the floor, and R.J. didn't see anything at first. Then he spotted some litter. "What's that?"

"Gum wrappers rolled up into small balls. Probably of clove-flavored gum."

"So?"

"We haven't given this out, but we've found the same thing at the places where two of the other women were attacked."

As R.J. realized what Russ was saying, he felt a surge of fear rip through him, but the fear wasn't for himself. All he could think of was how close this was to Lyndsey and how vulnerable she'd looked in sleep last night. It scared the hell out of him to think what could have happened. "You mean he was here in the hospital?"

Russ shrugged. "I don't know, but it's possible."

"Didn't anyone see him?"

"No," Russ said. "Let's get out of here." He moved out into the hallway, then said in a low voice, "This is just between us. We don't want it getting out. First thing you know, everyone who chews clove-flavored gum will be shot on sight."

R.J. nodded. "Sure." He looked down the hall at the single officer sitting in a chair by the door—the one Lyndsey was behind. "How could he have gotten this close?"

Russ began to walk down the hall, and R.J. fell in step beside him. "I don't know," Russ said. "But he won't get this close again."

R.J. stopped Russ with a hand on his arm. The large man turned to him. "Can you guarantee that?"

Russ looked right at R.J. "There're no guarantees in this life, but we'll do our very best."

R.J. dropped his hand, not feeling very reassured by the words. "Did you get anything from talking to her?"

"Bits and pieces. It's putting them together that's hard."

"She's almost ready to leave here, isn't she?" R.J. asked.

"Close."

"Then what?"

"We'll work that out. Until then, I'm depending on you to jog her memory."

"I'll try."

"Good. Good." They were just outside Lyndsey's door. "I'm going to make a call. I'll be back in a while if you need me."

R.J. nodded, then turned and reached out, touched the cold wood and pushed back the barrier to step into the hospital room. He took two steps inside before he saw the bed was empty, then he looked to the windows, expecting to see her there the way she'd been earlier, but she wasn't. The room was completely empty. Lyndsey was gone.

Chapter 6

R.J. knew a momentary fear that literally took his breath away, then he was responding on instinct. He called for the policeman outside the room and headed for the door. He didn't know what he was going to do, but he knew he had to find Lyndsey.

As he reached for the door, it swung toward him, striking his hand sharply, and he drew back as Russ ran into the room. At the same moment, the door to the bathroom opened and Lyndsey ran out into the room. R.J. stopped dead, staring at her, stunned by the sight and his monumental relief to see her unharmed. She was pulling a white terry-cloth robe around herself. Her hair clung to her head in a damp cap. "Wh-what?" she gasped as she fumbled in her pocket and took out her glasses.

"What in the hell?" Russ demanded, one hand holding the door open, the other resting on his holstered gun.

R.J. looked at Russ, then back at Lyndsey, who was slipping on her glasses. He was barely able to draw air into his tight lungs. God, he had never felt so terrified or so relieved in all of his life. And he wasn't fool enough to believe that if the woman standing unharmed in front of him was anyone else, he'd feel the same rush of emotions. No, he feared for Lyndsey Cole, and that fear went beyond his role as her psychiatrist.

"R.J., what happened?"

He tried to think straight. For three years he'd felt only one real, genuine emotion—grief. There wasn't room in him for these intense feelings that he knew could compromise him completely.

He shrugged, making himself take in air and look away from Lyndsey. "I...I didn't see..." He ran a hand over his face. "I'm sorry. I came in, and she wasn't here."

"I was trying to freshen up," Lyndsey said, and her husky voice ran havoc over his raw nerves.

He steeled himself, then turned back to her. As she knotted the tie at her waist and looked down so he didn't have to meet her gaze directly, he found it easier to speak. "I didn't know. I'm sorry if I scared you."

She looked up as her hands stilled, her eyes so blue they seemed the color of deep sapphires. "That's my perpetual state," she murmured and moved barefoot past R.J., stirring the air with soapy freshness. He found himself stepping back to put distance between them.

"You sure as hell scared me," Russ murmured.

R.J. turned back to the man. "Sorry. After what you found, I—" He cut off his words, but not fast enough.

"What did you find?" Lyndsey asked abruptly.

Russ looked at R.J., then past him to Lyndsey. "It looks as if the killer might have been in the hospital last night."

R.J. turned to Lyndsey, who was sitting on the side of the bed, her bare feet dangling above the tile floor. He could see the color draining from her face and her eyes widening. "What?"

Russ moved toward her, but R.J. didn't. He stayed where he was, certain if he went closer, he'd reach out to touch her, and he knew the folly of doing that again.

Russ held up a hand to her. "Listen, he wasn't close. Not at all, *if* it was him."

"What did he do?"

"Nothing. We just think he might have come into the hospital. We don't know for sure, and we won't for a while."

Lyndsey looked down at her hands which she'd clenched into fists on her thighs. Could Rob have gotten this close? It made her skin crawl just to think about how flimsy her protection could be if anyone was determined to get to her. "Do you think it was . . . whoever attacked me?" she asked in a small voice.

"It looks like it could have been, and that's why we need to get answers as quickly as possible. You and R.J. need to get to work. The sooner you remember, the sooner we can catch this guy."

Lyndsey looked up at Russ and adjusted her glasses, trying to hide how clearly his words were hitting their mark. He was right. She hadn't thought so until now, but he was dead right. She had to remember as soon as she could. If Rob had done this to her, she had to know. She had to make plans to run. If it wasn't Rob, then she had to give the police a description. "All right," she said and looked at R.J. "What do you want to do, and when do you want to start?"

She saw him hesitate, then he came closer. "We tried talking to jog your memory. That didn't work. So we're down to drugs or hypnosis. It's your choice."

"No drugs." She'd been unguarded enough last night with the painkiller. "I don't want to use drugs."

"Then hypnosis?"

She wasn't so sure about that, either. She didn't want to tell them about Rob, but she wanted to remember. "I don't know. I don't think—"

"You don't think what?"

"I've seen people hypnotized. They do things and say things . . ."

He came closer to stand by Russ. "Whatever you think you know about hypnosis, forget it. I'm a clinical hypnotherapist, not a performer in some lounge act in Las Vegas. My motivation isn't to get you to bark like a dog or for me to have total control over you. Hypnosis actually gives you the control. It lets you think without blocking your thoughts. It makes you free to remember without inhibitions."

He looked at her intently. "It's like watching a movie. You can see everything, maybe experience it if you want, but you'll tell me only what you want to tell me. You're the one in control. Not me."

How she longed to be in control again. "I won't do or say things I don't want to?"

"No, only what you feel right about saying or doing." He was very still. "Trust me," he said in a low voice.

In that moment she knew that despite everything, she did trust this man. What she felt on an emotional level when he was around was something she'd deal with later.

Right now she had to trust him. She touched her tongue to her lips and found the words. "All right. When can we start?"

"Right now," R.J. said. "I've had everything set up in my room."

Lyndsey found herself fingering the bruises on her right wrist. "Does this really work?"

"Sometimes it does. Sometimes it doesn't. Maybe we'll get lucky."

She nodded, but didn't say anything as Russ crossed to the connecting door and opened it. "We need all the luck we can get," he said.

Lyndsey slid off the side of the bed and steadied herself on the cool floor by touching the edge of the mattress.

"Let me help you," R.J. said softly, then touched her again, closing his fingers lightly around her upper arm. She welcomed the sudden heat in his touch, a heat she could feel clearly through the fabric of her robe. It seemed as if she had been cold for so long that she had been in danger of forgetting what warmth really was.

And R. J. Tyler seemed to be the one person in this whole crazy mess who could make her remember. She felt his body heat, and it brought comfort to her as she walked slowly toward the open door.

When she stepped into the next room, R.J. dropped his hold on her and went ahead of her past Russ. She followed him into a room that looked exactly like hers, except in one corner opposite the windows was an overstuffed reclining chair with a straight-backed chair beside it.

"Do you need anything else?" Russ asked.

"No, not for now," R.J. said.

"Russ," Lyndsey said before he could leave, "I really need some of my things from my apartment, some clothes and toiletries. If you could maybe get them?"

"Sure. I'll send someone over for you. Anything special?"

"In the bedroom dresser, there's underwear, some tops and jeans. Enough for a few days." Then she knew what she really needed. "And I was supposed to pick up my replacement contact lens on Monday. Do you think you could get it for me? The other lens is in a container in the medicine cabinet."

"I don't see why not. Just give me the doctor's name and address, and first thing in the morning, I'll get them and the clothes for you."

She gave him the information, then said, "I appreciate it."

Russ raked his fingers nervously through his hair. "I'll take care of everything for you, you just give this your best shot. You're the only hope we have right now for ending this nightmare."

She nodded, feeling her insides tighten even more at his words. Yes, she wanted an end to this nightmare, too. After she watched Russ leave, she looked up at R.J. "Just tell me what you want me to do."

He motioned to the reclining chair. "Sit down and make yourself as comfortable as possible."

She crossed to the chair and sat down, sinking slowly into the comfort of the soft corduroy-covered cushions. She eased back, felt the footrest pop out to support her legs and feet, then she turned to see R.J. sitting in a chair beside her.

"I'll explain everything I'm going to do," he said, his eyes hooded and unreadable. "First of all. Don't look at me. You know I'm here, and I won't let you forget it.

Just settle back, let your head rest on the chair back and don't cross your arms or legs. Let your hands rest open, palms down on the arms of the chair."

"Should I close my eyes?"

"If it feels right to close your eyes, do it. If not, don't. Take your glasses off or leave them on."

She slipped her glasses off, putting them in her lap, then she rested her hands on the arms of the chair and closed her eyes.

"Now, I'm going to touch you on your shoulder, Lyndsey," R.J. said softly.

She steeled herself for the contact, then felt it, a feather-light touch on her shoulder that brought the heat back, a heat that pushed the coldness in her a bit further away.

"Let your shoulders drop and relax," he said in a low voice that seemed to be surrounding her. "When you exhale, I'll press on your shoulder to help you, when you inhale, I'll ease up."

She let a breath out and felt the slight increase of pressure from his hand. Then she inhaled, and it eased. She exhaled and it came again.

"All right, Lyndsey, just listen and focus on my voice."

He didn't have to ask. His voice was already becoming the center of her consciousness.

"Think about a place where you've felt safe," R.J. said, "a place where you always knew you could relax and be at peace."

For a split second she was blank, thinking there had never been a place like that in her life. "It can be the mountains, the sea, the desert, a meadow," he said, and she remembered.

The sea. The ocean. The one summer when the world had begun to feel right, as if it was all coming into place. A perfect illusion that had lasted for two whole weeks during her sixteenth year when she'd met her parents in the south of Spain.

"Can you visualize a place?"

She started to talk, but he stopped her with increased pressure on her shoulder.

"Don't talk just yet. Relax and let your thoughts flow. Let me know your answers by lifting your right index finger for yes, your left for no. Can you visualize a place?"

She raised her right finger.

"The mountains?"

She raised her left finger.

"The sea?"

She raised her right finger.

"All right. Now make that place as perfect as you can. The waves are gentle, the sand white and clean, the air so clear you can see forever."

As he spoke, the feeling of him being close to her slipped away to be replaced by his voice as her companion. That was her only conscious awareness of anything beyond her own thoughts—a voice that almost seemed as if it was coming from inside herself.

She could see the ocean, the small house on the bluffs her parents had rented for those two weeks, a tiny place, white and clean. And the water flowing onto the sands, swirling around her bare feet, the heat of the sun on her face. She did feel safe, and she felt a peacefulness that she knew could bring tears if she let herself dwell on the sensation.

"Is everything perfect?" R.J. asked.

"Yes," she whispered, needing to speak and not use her fingers for the response.

"Now that you have this safe place, remember it. Memorize it. And you know you can always go back to it no matter how awful things get for you. Do you understand that?"

"Yes."

"Now, try to remember Friday, two days ago. It's morning, clear, October, almost Indian summer. Can you remember it?"

This isn't like Seattle, she'd thought as she woke that morning. She'd heard it was never really warm here, but it had been. And so beautiful. She'd almost decided to walk to work, to enjoy the day and her freedom. "Yes, I remember."

"Now, it's up to you, Lyndsey. Do you want to be in this memory and experience it, or do you want to watch it, as if it's a movie you're starring in, and you're watching it being shown in a theater?"

"Just . . . just watch," she murmured, sensing it was safer for her that way.

"All right. Picture that day in your mind. See the morning. See yourself there as the day begins."

Her images shifted and she saw herself, watching the images in front of her from the shadows, and the voice of R.J. all around. She was coming out of her apartment dressed in a straight gray linen skirt with a matching jacket, a white silk blouse with a cowled neckline and her hair skimmed back from her face into a twist. She had her purse, her glasses on, and the door of the apartment was closing behind her.

"What are you doing?" the voice asked inside her.

"Leaving my apartment."

"Where are you going?"

"To. . . to get my car and go to work."

"Skip ahead, go through the day. Fast forward the picture until you're at lunch. What's going on now?"

She was in the pink-and-beige office of the optometrist getting tested for her replacement contact. "I'm at the eye doctor's. He's testing me. He says he'll rush my new lens."

"Have you seen anyone, or have you talked to anyone there who makes you uncomfortable?"

"No, not at all."

"Then fast forward and you're back at work. Is there anything there that bothers you?"

She loved her job. It was what she'd wanted to do all along, and she actually enjoyed going in each day. "No, nothing bothers me."

"Fast forward again until you're about to leave work."

She felt in control as her day slipped past in a blur. She felt safe. As long as the voice was there, she knew she was all right. Now it was late afternoon. She was outside the building where she worked, leaving, going to the parking area near the Sound under the cement arched trestles that weaved over the area. The sun was clear, but it was getting cooler, the air clean, the city alive.

"Where are you?" R.J. asked.

"Outside. Going to the car."

"Just tell me what you want to let me know."

"I. . . I'm leaving work. I have to get my car and go."

"Go where?"

"To the bank."

"You're heading for the car. Are you talking to anyone?"

"No. Just thinking."

"About what?"

She couldn't say the words. Instead, she murmured, "Things."

"Are you at the car yet?"

She watched her image in front of her get to the lot, nod to the attendant, give him the voucher, then go to the car. "Yes."

"Inside it?"

She got in. "Yes."

"Are you going to the bank now?"

She watched herself driving through the traffic, stopping at the bank, getting out, going in. "Yes. I'm there."

"Is there anything wrong now?"

"No, no." She was coming out of the bank, back to the car. Someone knocked her arm as she passed by, knocking her glasses off, then she was picking them up and going on. She didn't look back. She was at the car, inside, starting it, driving off.

"What's going on now?"

"I'm driving."

"Where are you driving to?"

"To my apartment."

"How do you feel?"

"Tired."

"What are you thinking?"

"I wish I hadn't torn my contact lens. I hate my glasses."

"Where are you?"

She was on the street, pulling left to go into the underground parking area. She knew she was watching a movie, that she wasn't really there, yet she could feel the first shards of fear. If the movie kept going, if the car went underground into the parking area, if she drove into her space, if she stopped the motor, if she sat in the silence looking at herself in the mirror, if she opened the door...

"Where are you, Lyndsey?" R.J.'s voice asked her again.

"In the car...going into park..."

"Tell me what's happening."

With a jolt she knew she wasn't watching a movie anymore. She was in it, right in the middle, experiencing it all, and she found it hard to say anything. "The...the car stops. I sit there. I look in the mirror. I touch the door handle. Oh, God, I can't," she gasped. "I can't."

"Yes, you can," the voice urged her.

She knew she'd explode into a million pieces if she kept going. "No, please, no."

"It's all right, Lyndsey. You're safe. You can go back to the safe place any time you want to. Do you understand that?"

"Please, I...I want back," she said as she felt the cold metal of the handle under her fingers. The door was clicking open. "Please, help me."

"*You* have to do it," R.J. said. "You have to make yourself go back to the safe place. Just do it."

The door was opening for Lyndsey, her feet swinging out to strike the cement. "No," she said.

"The safe place, Lyndsey, go to it," R.J. was whispering to her. The safe place. The safe place. She chanted it in her mind, letting R.J.'s voice mingle with her own.

"The safe place," R.J.'s voice was echoing in her. "Now, Lyndsey, now!"

And she was suddenly at the ocean, the sand, the sun, the safety, the rhythm of the tides, and R.J.'s voice all around her. "You're all right. You're safe. You can't be hurt here. You know that, don't you?"

Yes, she did. She knew as long as R.J. was there, talking, and the safe place was all around her, she was all right.

"Do you know that?" he asked again.

"Yes," she whispered. "Yes."

"All right. Relax. Let it wash over you. Just be there."

R.J.'s voice seemed to fill her and heal her. And she could feel the fear draining from her, seeping away to some dark place that couldn't touch her here.

"Now, I'll count backward from five, and you can open your eyes any time you want to. Five."

There was just the voice, but it was beginning to change, to leave the inside of her to surround her being.

"Four."

She could feel her body resting in the chair, the coolness of air on her arms and feet, and a sense of sorrow that she had to leave the safe place.

"Three."

Reality was there, just seconds away, a time when she would lose this sense of safety and peace, and another, more subtle fear began to touch her as she knew she had to face reality.

"Two."

The safe place was dissolving, almost gone as if it had never been, and Lyndsey fought it. She didn't want to come back to this world, to face what she knew was waiting for her.

"One."

It was gone. She was in the chair, breathing evenly and very alone in her thoughts. Yet the sense of R.J. being there was still strong and compelling. She wasn't quite alone physically, and she didn't want to open her eyes.

"Are you awake?" he asked softly.

"Yes." Her voice sounded low and slurred.

"Open your eyes whenever you want to, but while you're resting, let your mind just wander. Don't try to remember, but let your thoughts flow. Be open to anything that comes to you."

She let her thoughts drift, nothing really forming, yet she sensed that they were going someplace. They slipped from here to there, skimming over reality, edging away from the past, away from her time with Rob, then she knew her thoughts were zeroing in on R. J. Tyler. That realization stopped her, and she made herself open her eyes.

The room was softly lit, the blinds closed, yet she didn't remember R.J. ever closing them. She didn't have to look to know he was still there, in the chair, silent, waiting. "It was a failure, wasn't it?" she breathed.

"No. You were approaching the incident. It's hard. It isn't something that just happens, but we'll try again."

"When?"

Before R.J. could answer, the connecting door from the next room opened and Lyndsey put on her glasses, then looked to her left to see Russ stride into the room. He looked from Lyndsey to R.J., then asked, "Are you done?"

"For now."

Lyndsey watched Russ, sensing even more agitation and nervousness in him than there had been before, and it was all mingled with what she knew without asking was real anger. "Did she remember anything?"

"No, not this time."

He came closer and looked down at Lyndsey. "I can't deal in lies, Lyndsey. They can't be tolerated, not when your life and others' lives depend on the truth."

She could feel the anger directed at her, and she had no idea what he was talking about. She sat up, pushing the footrest down, and she nervously fingered the tie to her robe. The soft terry cloth twisted around her fingers, and she felt as if this world held little of what she knew or understood. "I understand that."

"Then why did you lie to me?"

She could feel the blood draining from her face. Oh, God, he knew about Rob. She looked at R.J. Had he told Russ? She felt betrayed and foolish to have thought that R.J. would keep what she'd said between them. After all, he worked for the police, not for her.

"I...I don't know what you're talking about." She bluffed, hoping against hope that he was talking about something else.

"What are you talking about, Russ?" R.J. asked.

Russ glanced at R.J., a slanting look from angry eyes. "And you were worried about how to handle her, how to deal with her. She's been lying. Flat out lying to us."

"Lying? About what?" R.J. asked.

"She's not alone, and she tried to contact someone this morning by phone before we went in to see her."

She felt a degree of relief that R.J. hadn't told him anything. That meant a lot to her. When she'd made those calls, she hadn't even thought about the police checking on her. It really made her feel like a prisoner. "I just said there was no one to contact," she said quickly.

R.J. looked at Lyndsey and didn't have to ask what was going on. Her husband. He hadn't told Russ about the man, sensing that Lyndsey didn't want anyone to know about him. But why would Lyndsey want to get in touch with the man after what he'd done to her? "You made a call?"

She bit her lip and nodded. "Yes."

R.J. could feel the intensity in Russ, and flinched as he bit out each word. "She called a Rob Peters in Dallas, at his home and at his place of work. Do you want to tell me who he is, Lyndsey?"

Lyndsey paled, and the peacefulness that R.J. had sensed in her during their session was gone completely. She wrapped her arms around herself protectively and stared at Russ, her lips working, but nothing came. And in that instant, R.J. knew such a need to protect her that it staggered him. To protect her from Russ? God, that didn't make sense, not Russ, the man he'd known for most of his life, the one person on this earth he considered a real friend. Yet it was there, and he knew he'd do battle with Russ to stop him from damaging Lyndsey any further.

"You know, don't you?" she finally managed in a low, unsteady voice.

"Know what?" Russ demanded.

"He was my husband, but we're divorced. It's over."

Russ got closer to her. "Then why in the hell did you try to reach him?"

She shook her head. "I don't know. I just..." She looked at R.J. "I felt alone. I didn't think."

He understood that need to have someone, anyone. If he didn't have Russ, if he was totally alone, would he reach out to anyone who came by? He didn't know.

"Damn it, Lyndsey," Russ ground out. "I—"

R.J. moved abruptly, stepping between Russ and Lyndsey as a shield for her from the man's burning anger. And this time it wasn't a question of good guy-bad guy, it was purely an instinctive move to protect her from a man who had always been like a brother to him. A man who was becoming precariously close to being the enemy.

"Hold on, Russ." He held up both hands palms-out in front of him to fend off the verbal attack. "Stop it right there."

Russ narrowed his eyes, then took a step back, but he didn't back down in his tone or words. "Don't tell me what to do. Remember, you work for us, R.J."

"Then let me do my job. Let me do it my way. That doesn't include you coming in here like some mad bull ready to tear up a china shop."

Russ was still, then his eyes narrowed as he muttered tightly, "He's killed again."

R.J. felt his heart lurch. "What?"

"Early this morning. A woman near the aquarium, lived alone, thirty-one, blond, blue-eyed, etcetera, etcetera."

R.J. had the biting impression that the big man in front of him was about to explode into a million pieces. He was wound as tight as a coiled spring. "Are you sure it's the same man?"

"Damn right," Russ muttered, then he turned and crossed to the windows, his back to the room and the two people in it.

R.J. glanced down at Lyndsey, who was still in the chair. Her face was chalk-white, her eyes behind the lenses wide and filled with fear.

He looked back at the big man. "I understand, Russ, you know I do, but don't do this now," he said.

"What do you suggest I do?" he demanded harshly without turning. "While she lies to us, women are dying, and if she's lied about this, what else has she lied about?" He spun around, his gaze pinning Lyndsey.

"How about it? Are you lying about seeing the killer? Would you even tell us if you had seen him?"

She scrambled to her feet, almost bumping into R.J. in the process. But she wasn't looking at him. She was staring at Russ. "You think that I saw him, and that I'm lying about that?"

"That possibility has crossed my mind more than once."

The cord to her robe was being twisted tightly around her hand, over and over again, and R.J. was so close to her that he could hear her inhale jerkily before she spoke. "Why would I do that?"

"You told me you were alone in the world, that you had no one at all, just your parents overseas. That there was no one here to notify."

"I know, but it didn't seem important to say anything about Rob," she said.

"What else haven't you told us because it 'didn't seem important'?"

R.J. saw her almost flinch, and he was struck by how delicate she looked in the skimpy robe with her feet bare. "I swear, I can't remember. There's no face in my mind," she whispered. "I swear that's the truth."

R.J. reached out when he saw Lyndsey tremble, touching her on the shoulder, and it unsettled him to feel the unsteadiness in her. "That's enough, Russ." He paused, then repeated for emphasis, "Enough."

"Not nearly enough," Russ muttered, then strode across the room, past the two people and out the corridor door.

R.J. watched the door close behind Russ, then he looked down at Lyndsey. The sight of her struck at a chord deep in his soul. She was alone, totally alone, and trying to keep her abusive husband as far from her thoughts and life as possible. Yet she'd called him. It didn't make sense, but not for the reasons Russ thought.

"Why did you call your ex-husband?" he asked, needing to know.

Lyndsey didn't say a thing. She closed her eyes for a fleeting moment, then shrugged, a faint, unsteady motion that tore at R.J. He felt so many things when this woman was this close, things he couldn't begin to define, or maybe he didn't want to define. Rage at the husband was so easy to deal with, so simple, compared to looking at Lyndsey and feeling a flood of need that had no place in the reality of the situation.

He'd felt nothing like this for so long, then it was there. Just a look from Lyndsey, a glance from the deep blue depths of her eyes, or the slight unsteadiness of her full bottom lip. Physical deprivation. That's what it was, he decided. Physically being alone for so long was playing havoc with his hormones and his body. But even as he made his own explanations for the fire beginning to grow in him, he knew there was more to it, and that fact really shook him.

Then, as she silently stared up at him, he moved his hand from her shoulder to her chin, to gently cup the sweep of her jaw, touching the silky heat of her skin.

Lyndsey was in strange waters. She'd never felt protected before in her life. She'd never felt as if someone was unerringly on her side, ready to step between her and threatening havoc. And she didn't know how to react to what R.J. had just done. Her emotions were scrambled, yet intense. In one instant, she felt such a connection with this man that it took her breath away, and in the next, she felt a response to his touch on her that couldn't begin to be understood.

And he'd protected her, not even telling Russ about Rob's abuse or their split. It was too much to take in, and her only clear thought was she wished she'd met this man years ago, before there had been a Rob in her life, and that she could hold on to him forever and never let go.

"Thank you for not telling him about Rob." His fingers moved on her skin, and she could barely find the words she needed to say. "He's got a right to be angry. I just couldn't tell him about Rob. I wish I could remember," she said in an annoyingly unsteady voice. "But I . . . I can't. I swear. That's not a lie."

"I know," he murmured. "I believe you."

"I need to know who did this to me. I really need . . ."

He understood need completely, when all he could think about at that moment was his need to taste her lips, to hold her body against his to see how it fit against his angles, and to feel her heat mingle with his. Rationally he knew he should break his hold on her, that he should turn and get the hell out of the room, but there was nothing rational in him when he lowered his head to taste her lips with his. And when he made contact, he wasn't prepared for the intensity of the sensations that shot through him, shaking him to the core of his being.

Chapter 7

Lyndsey felt as if she had been cold all of her life, not just these past few days. And when R.J.'s lips touched hers, she finally understood the meaning of body heat. She leaned toward him, letting her body press to his, and she took his heat, opening her mouth to it, needing the heat to survive.

She didn't bother to wonder what she was doing, or why she was doing it, she just knew that every nerve of her body was alive and bathed in a fire that didn't burn, but brought life with it. She slid her hands around him, holding him, in mortal fear of him leaving her when she was just beginning to find her own soul. His tongue tested her lips, parting them gently, then flashing inside to roam over the contours of her mouth, teasing her tongue.

From nowhere, there came flashes of memory and a strange comparison—Rob with the hard lips and punishing touches, his teeth grating on hers, then R.J. with the gentle touch, and the heat. It was a combination she'd never experienced before. Yet she knew that combination had the power to exorcise demons in her.

She clung to R.J., desperate for what he had, and desperate with wanting to know more fire than she ever had before. She wanted that with a deep ache born out of a lifetime of deprivation. She felt his hips pressed to hers, and she knew that his need was as great as her own.

R.J. held Lyndsey with a desperation he'd never experienced before. She felt as light and fragile as a butterfly in his hold, yet her response to him was anything but uncertain. He felt his needs growing with a speed that left him breathless. Her mouth was so damned irresistible, her taste as unique as anything in this world, and her robe a fragile covering for her mysteries.

Then he felt his own trembling, his own insatiable desire that ripped through him, and it stopped him cold. Desperation was making him do things he wouldn't have considered forty-eight hours ago. This was a lunacy that he couldn't follow through with, no matter how great his need. No, he instinctively knew if he got closer to this woman, he'd be lost. And when she was gone, he wouldn't have anything left, not professionally, not personally.

With all the determination he could muster, R.J. took hold of her arms and moved her away from him. He couldn't go through with this at all.

Lyndsey was jarred back to her senses when R.J. broke his hold on her, and she was more embarrassed than she'd ever been in her life. He knew about Rob. And he probably thought she was the most desperate woman in the world. God knows she was acting like it, clinging to him like some teenager in the first throes of puppy love. And that's exactly how she felt. And as foolish. This man had known love, a great love, according to Russ, and he'd never love like that again. Love? That didn't even enter into this. That last thought brought back all the coldness in her.

"I'm sorry," she whispered, avoiding eye contact as she reached for the back of the reclining chair to keep herself steady. Her legs were like jelly. "I'm sorry," she repeated and headed for the adjoining door to make her escape. She just prayed her legs would carry her for that far without giving out.

"Lyndsey?" she heard R.J. say when she was at the door.

She touched the knob for support and didn't turn. "What?"

"That won't happen again," he said.

"No, it won't," she said, then turned the knob and went into her room. She closed the door behind her and leaned back against the coolness of the wooden barrier. No, it wouldn't happen again.

R.J. stood very still as he fought the urge to go after her. He couldn't. What else could he say to her? There was nothing he could say to explain what he'd allowed to happen. And there was no way he could explain his guilt at taking advantage of her. Just because he needed the contact, that didn't mean that he could act on his impulses.

He turned and headed for the corridor door. He needed to breathe air that wasn't saturated with the scent of Lyndsey. And he needed to put as much distance as he could between himself and the chance of making another mistake.

B & B Strangler Strikes Again. Fourth Victim Still in Coma. No Clue To Motives. Police Still Baffled.

The lone man in the hospital maintenance coveralls read the headlines through the plastic shield of the newspaper vending machines by the entrance of Blair Memorial.

The motives were so simple. He didn't understand why they didn't realize what was going on. She was blond and blue-eyed and beautiful, and he wanted her.

He narrowed his eyes as he backed up enough to scan the sheer front of the glass-and-steel structure and pick out the tenth-floor windows. The glass hid everything, glinting back the clear noontime sunlight.

They didn't understand how the look in her eyes, the blueness flooded with heat and the desire deep in them, had turned cold. Heat that drew him like a moth to flame had turned to a chill that killed all the promises. She'd turned from him, her hair feathered around her face, her chin held high. She'd turned away and left him.

He couldn't take that. He wouldn't take that. He had a fear of rejection, of desertion, some therapist had told him once. But that wasn't all that fed this rage in him. It was her not wanting him. It was simple.

He stared at the windows, his hands clenched so tightly they were almost numb. The cops were on her floor, and one had been stationed at the main entrance, checking as unobtrusively as possible when anyone went in. But they didn't even bother him. A janitor could go anywhere he wanted to go. When the elevator doors had opened last night, when he'd come face-to-face with the cop, nothing had happened. They'd talked, then the cop had even wished him a very pleasant "good evening" before the doors closed.

He smiled and headed up the steps to the entrance. He'd get up to the tenth floor again, and this time, he'd get to her room. He wouldn't stand in the stairwell for hours and get nowhere. And she wouldn't ever know what had happened. She just wouldn't wake up from the coma. Then it would be over and done, and he could get on with his life.

He pulled back the door and stepped inside, almost running into a man hurrying outside. He sidestepped, muttering a profanity that didn't faze the tall man in the blue sports coat with gray streaked hair. The man never turned, never acknowledged the near collision as he strode down the steps and out into the sunlight.

He hated people who acted as if he didn't exist, but before he could focus much anger on the stranger, he saw the cop in the lobby looking at him. He smiled, nodded to the man, then strode with assurance toward the back of the lobby and the service area, his mind totally focused on what he had to do. He'd kill her this time, he thought, and the idea made him feel alive.

R.J. spotted Russ getting into a squad car near the side parking lot entrance of the hospital, and he broke into a jog. "Russ!"

The big man turned at the sound of his name, and he held the car door open with one hand. "What do you want?" he asked abruptly as R.J. stopped in front of him.

"I understand that you're edgy and upset, but I'm asking you to lay off Lyndsey. She's got enough horror in her life without you badgering her."

Russ looked at R.J. long and hard, then asked, "Why was she calling her ex-husband?"

"She needed a connection. She's afraid, alone, and needed to make contact with someone she used to know, an anchor to reality, I guess you could call it."

Russ fingered the cool metal of the door top, the light wind off the Sound ruffling his hair. "Do you buy that?"

R.J. didn't know what he bought anymore, but he nodded anyway. "It makes sense."

"Whatever you say."

"Where are you going now?" R.J. asked.

"To the morgue. The preliminary report's ready on the last victim. I need to see it and talk to the examiner." He slid into the squad car, but before he closed the door, he looked out and up at R.J. "Where are you off to?"

R.J. had no idea. "Out. I need to take care of things," he said with deliberate vagueness.

"What about the convention?"

"It's off. I told them I wouldn't be able to make it at all."

"Too bad. I know you were looking forward to it."

R.J. almost agreed, then stopped himself. He hadn't really been looking forward to the convention, but to the escape it represented for him. It had never been viewed by him as pleasure, not even as a source of mental stimulation. He found himself halfheartedly nodding to Russ and murmuring, "Yeah, I was," as he realized he hadn't given the convention cancellation a second thought once he'd decided to stay and help Lyndsey.

"You coming back here soon?" Russ asked.

"Yeah, soon," R.J. said and walked away, without an idea of where he was going, only that he had to get the taste of Lyndsey off his lips, and the memory of the feel of her in his arms, out of his mind.

When R.J. walked into Lyndsey's room just before dinner, he found her sitting cross-legged on the bed, dressed in worn jeans, a loose white shirt with the collar done up to cover the mark of the rope at her throat, and her feet bare. She had combed her hair, and there was a touch of color on her lips. Her eyes were as wide and as blue as he remembered and just as capable of scrambling his thoughts.

Looking away from her gaze, he closed the door and crossed to the bed. Then he steeled himself and looked at her again. "It's my turn to say I'm sorry," he said before he could think twice about it.

He saw color touch her cheeks, and she lowered her eyes to her hands that were worrying the untucked hem of her shirt. He wished he'd just ignored the kiss instead of bringing it up. But now he had to follow through.

"It...it's this..." She moved her shoulders in a faint shrug. "It's crazy, and people act differently when they're under stress, don't they?"

He knew he did. And he knew that the desire to touch her was just as strong as it had been hours ago before he'd driven back to his apartment, gone through tons of paperwork, and walked aimlessly down by Pike Market on the Sound. "Yes, I guess they do," he murmured.

She looked up at him and adjusted her glasses with her forefinger pressed to the nosepiece. "It's over and done," she said, her voice flat and her eyes unreadable.

"Yes, it is," he lied, then quickly changed the subject. "I didn't mean to leave you alone for so long, but I had work to do. Has Russ been back?"

She grimaced and spread her hands to either side, cutting them in an arch through the air. "No one's been here but the man who brought me my clothes and the officer who came in and told me not to watch television or listen to the radio." She pointed to the television suspended from the wall near the ceiling across from the foot of the bed. "And I haven't turned that thing on."

"I called to ask him to tell you. I thought it was best if you didn't."

"I know." She sighed. "What have you been doing all day?"

He slipped off his jacket and lay it over the back of the chair by the bed, then he turned and shoved his hands into the pockets of his slacks. "Just catching up on work at my office."

"I thought Russ said you didn't have office hours?"

"Oh, he did, did he?"

"Well, he said you had flexible hours."

"I have those, all right." He rocked forward on the balls of his feet. "I was getting paperwork done. I have an office, but I mostly do research and consultations now."

"Like my case?"

"No. I haven't done something like this for... for a while."

"What nationality are you?" she asked him out of the blue.

He rocked back on his heels. "What?"

"Where did your ancestors come from?"

"Ireland and England, with a slice of Apache Indian somewhere in the deep, dark past."

"Mmm," she said, her eyes narrowing as she openly studied him. "All right. Rutherford Jean."

He shook his head. "Pardon me?"

"Your name, is that it?"

"No," he said, feeling an easy smile lift his lips, an expression that was very welcome. "Not even close."

She cocked her head to one side. "How about Rodney Jerome?"

"Where are you getting these ideas?"

"I figure your name has to be really different, or you'd tell me and you wouldn't be using your initials. So..."

"I'll give you some help." He could deal with this teasing much more easily than any other phase of his relationship with Lyndsey. "My family settled in Texas long before I was born, and I lived there until I was ten years old."

"That's a big help." She smiled, a lovely expression that softened her face and made her even more beautiful. "Then we could be talking something like Robbie Joe Tyler, or Ray Jay Tyler, couldn't we?"

R.J. laughed at that, and it felt good to express some emotion other than what he'd been feeling these past hours. "We could be, but we aren't," he finally managed to say.

"Darn," she muttered, her face puckered in a frown. "This is frustrating."

"Why do you need to know my name?"

She looked at him, the laughter dying. "I think I'm entitled to know the real name of someone who's trying to look into my mind."

"I don't know—"

He was cut off when the door opened and the same nurse who had been there that morning came in with a tray of food. "Dinnertime," she said with her unflagging cheerfulness.

She came across the room, put the tray on the table that swung across the bed, then looked at Lyndsey. "Enough food for both of you here. Are you ready to eat?"

"I sure am," Lyndsey said, sitting back and tugging the table across the bed. She lifted one of the metal covers and sighed. "Hamburgers and french fries. Cholesterol and fat, it looks terrific."

"This isn't usual hospital fare, but we thought you'd enjoy something we call comfort food." The nurse helped her adjust the table. "Now, is there anything else you need?"

Lyndsey looked at R.J. "Anything special you need?"

He hadn't thought about food all day, but now his stomach felt decidedly empty. "No, I'm easy to please. Hamburgers and fries sounds just fine."

She looked at the nurse. "Thanks for this. I appreciate it."

"You enjoy it," the nurse said, then left.

As the door closed, Lyndsey looked at R.J. and motioned to the tray. "Here's your plate."

R.J. sank into the chair by the bed and took the plate of food that Lyndsey held out to him. "Can you swallow all right?"

Her expression faltered as her hand lifted to her throat covered by the high neck of the shirt. Then she shrugged. "The doctor says I'm as good as new. No problems, other than a madman trying to kill me."

The forced joke fell flat, and they looked at each other for a long moment. Then R.J. stood and put his plate on the side table. "Eat up. I'll be right back," he said as he crossed to the connecting door and left.

Lyndsey watched the door shut behind him, then she sank back in the bed, her appetite waning rapidly. How could she be so pleased to see him, then make such a fool of herself? She picked up a french fry and tasted it, chewing slowly. There was no point in remembering what had happened between them earlier. No point to it at all.

She'd gone over and over it in her mind all day, sorting through it, trying to forget her reactions to R.J.'s kiss, and telling herself that it had meant nothing. She didn't want a relationship, never again, and especially not with a man who was still in love with his dead wife. And she knew that R.J. had acted impulsively, probably feeling sorry for her. That made sense, and she thought she'd sorted that out and put it behind her.

Then he'd walked into the room, with the scent of fresh air clinging to him, his hair windblown and his lean build clearly defined in slim slacks, the pale shirt and deep blue jacket. She'd tried to make small talk, teased him about his name, then told a joke that fell horribly flat.

She looked at the french fry and dropped it on the plate. She had her own clothes and would have her contacts soon. Physically she was doing fine. Other than having a killer after her, or her crazy ex-husband trying to kill her, she was doing just great.

"What a mess," she muttered, and reached for the glass of milk on her tray. Then she noticed the local paper the nurse had folded neatly and set under her plate. She hadn't turned on the television or the radio all day in case the news on them affected the way she remembered. But no one had mentioned the newspaper. She considered not looking at it, then she moved the plate just a bit, and she clearly saw part of a headline that started "B & B Strangler..." That was enough for her to reach for it with an annoyingly unsteady hand.

She opened the paper to read the main item on the top center of the front page. Three separate articles were there, one on the most recent death with a blurred picture of a woman with pale hair and small features. The second item was on the other attacks, and as she skimmed the text, she saw that her name wasn't there, just the innocuous, "the unidentified fourth victim is still in a coma." She looked to the third article, skimmed it and stopped dead at the word "raped" in the second paragraph.

She stared at the single word. She'd never even thought about her attack beyond the pain she'd endured and the fact either the killer or Rob was still out there. Raped? Her stomach churned, and she had to close her eyes to settle herself. But it didn't help at all. If the killer had raped the women, if he was the one who had attacked her and not Rob...? Had she been raped?

The door opened and she jerked her head to her right. R.J. strode back into the room, and as he looked at her, he stopped dead and asked, "What is it?"

She waved one hand in the air, then pushed the food tray back so abruptly that the milk slopped over the sides of the glass. She scrambled to the edge of the bed, but didn't have anywhere to go. She stared at R.J. as he came closer.

"Lyndsey, what's wrong?" he asked, then he moved abruptly and reached for the newspaper. "You were reading this?"

She nodded, unable to say anything.

"Damn it!" He looked at the items, then back at her as he tossed the paper into the trash basket by the bed. "What did you read? What's got you so scared?"

She tried to say the words, but had to try twice before they would come out with any coherency. "Was...was I raped?"

He was so still that for an instant she had the horrifying feeling she had been raped and no one had told her. Sickness rose in her throat, then as she swallowed, R.J. came closer still, reaching out to take her by her upper arms. He got his face within inches of hers and said in a low voice, "No, you weren't raped. None of the women were. That report is pure speculation."

"Are . . . are you sure?"

"Absolutely. The police didn't tell the press specifics about the attacks. They didn't want to put them out in case some creep took to duplicating them for publicity." His hold on her was firm, but reassuring. "You know that some people do copycat crimes. They didn't want that, so they didn't give out particulars. One of those particulars was that none of the women were sexually molested."

She stared at R.J.

"Russ has the idea that the guy is impotent, or at least has problems with his sexuality."

Lyndsey felt the world begin to recede as Rob's words echoed in her mind. "It's you, Lyndsey, it's not me. I never had problems with a woman in my life until you started to complain about everything. If you were sexier, I'd be fine."

She tried to take in a breath, anything to stop the voices in her head. "Impotent?"

"Or so angry he can't do anything."

Angry? "It's you, not me!" Rob had screamed at her as he got out of bed, then in the darkness he'd turned on her. "It's your fault," he'd said in a cold, hard voice, then he'd struck out.

She closed her eyes tightly, and she felt R.J.'s hold on her tighten just a bit as he shook her gently. "Lyndsey, forget about it."

She opened her eyes and met with the deep caring in his gaze. "Tell me how to forget."

"You weren't raped. You were violated, but not sexually. And you survived. That has to be enough for now,

until we can find the man who hurt you and make him
pay for what he did." His hands moved up until they
were cupping her face, his touch hot on her cold skin.
"Trust me, Lyndsey. I'm telling you the truth. And I
promise you we'll get him. He'll be locked away for the
rest of his life."

She looked into his eyes and knew that trusting him
was almost as easy for her now as loving him could be.
That stopped everything for her. Love? No. She'd never
known it, and she never would. Life was simpler that
way, safer. Besides, how could she even recognize love
it it came to her? She'd thought she loved Rob. Now she
knew she hated him. No, she wouldn't know love. What
R. J. Tyler made her feel was something physical,
something a teenager could deal with easier than she
could right now.

She moved back, away from R.J.'s touch, scooting
back until she was against the raised back of the bed. But
she *would* deal with it. The way she did everything else.
With an unsteady hand, she swiped at her face, then
looked at R.J. Yes, she could deal with this. "Do you
really think they'll catch him?"

"I'd put my money on the cops." He reached for her
tray and swung it across her lap again. "Russ is like a
maniac until he has answers." He stood back and smiled
a bit sheepishly at her. "You know how he can act."

"Yes, I do," she said, fingering the edge of the metal
table.

"Now, you need to eat. You need food."

She stared down at the plate, the idea of eating the
furthest thing from her mind right then, but she reached
for a french fry and took a bite. As she chewed, she tried
to remember the last time food had tasted good to her.
Then she knew. The day of the attack. She'd gone to

lunch by herself at a small Mexican restaurant someone at work had told her about. An eternity ago.

She swallowed and looked up at R.J. who hadn't moved. "Aren't you going to eat your food?"

R.J. reached for the plate on the side table. Raped? God, the idea made his stomach churn with a sickness that he thought would never settle. He looked down at the plate of food. He should have thought about the newspaper. A mistake. He'd make sure that no other newspaper got in here. After he sat down, he rested the plate on his lap and picked up his hamburger. He took a bite and found it was flat and the french fries were barely warm.

For several minutes, he picked at the food, never looking at Lyndsey. When he couldn't swallow another bite, he put the plate back on the table, dropped a napkin over the uneaten food so he wouldn't have to look at it, then sat back in the chair with a grimace. When he glanced at Lyndsey, she was watching him with a hint of humor that put a provocative light in the blueness of her eyes.

"You're amused?" he asked as he settled, lifting one leg to rest his ankle on the opposite knee.

"You looked at the food as if it was the most awful thing you've ever seen." She glanced at her own plate that was almost empty. "It's pretty bad, but it's not poison." She looked at him again. "Food isn't one of your passions, is it?"

The word passion was all he heard for a moment, wondering if she could read minds and know that passion wasn't too far from the surface when he looked at her. "Food? No, I guess not. Food isn't that important to me, to tell you the truth."

"You eat to live instead of living to eat?"

He shrugged and lifted one eyebrow. "I live. I eat. I guess the two go together in some basic, metabolic way."

"That's a pretty bleak rationale," she said as she pushed at her tray to swing it away from the bed.

"Life's pretty bleak at times," he muttered, then glanced at his watch. "Do you feel up to trying to find some answers? It's only seven o'clock."

She moved further back and looked at him intently, the blueness of her eyes deep and pure against her pale skin. "I don't have any plans for this evening," she said. "Your place or mine?"

"I've got the chairs," he said.

"Then we may as well use your room," she said as she slid off the bed and went past him to the adjoining door. Without looking back, she went into his room, and R.J. followed her, pausing just long enough to turn off the overhead lights to leave the room lit by one side light.

He turned and saw Lyndsey was already in the easy chair, leaning back with the footrest up, and looking at him from under her ridiculously long lashes. "Whenever you're ready," she murmured. "Let's get this over with."

He came across, sat by her in the straight-backed chair, then spoke softly. "It's the same as before. I'll sit here, touch your shoulder and talk to you. All you need to do is go back to that safe place you made for yourself this morning. All right?"

She nodded, settling back with her eyes closed. R.J. held out his hand, almost touching her shoulder, but he hesitated. It took a real determination to touch her, to make himself put his hand on her, to feel her softness under his fingers, and make himself think only professional thoughts. This is important, he told himself. It's a job. Sure, and pigs fly, he thought wryly, and exhaled.

Lyndsey felt his touch on her, welcoming it this time, making it easier for her to lower her shoulders and breathe deeply.

"Just let go, Lyndsey, and drift to the safe place you created the first time," R.J. said softly. "Just relax and let yourself drift. Go further and further, until you're in your safe place."

At the sound of his words, Lyndsey did as he said, slipping further and further away from reality until she felt herself nearing the safe place. Then she was there, at the ocean, feeling the silky sand under her feet, the heat on her face, the freedom, the peace. And R.J.'s voice seemed to be everywhere.

"Are you where you want to be?" he asked.

"Yes," she said, feeling the absolute truth of the single word she uttered.

"Now, when you shift to last Friday this time, do you want to watch or be in the picture?"

She didn't want to shift. She never wanted to.

"Lyndsey, do you want to watch or be in the picture?" R.J. was asking again.

"I can't leave here."

"Why can't you? Is someone keeping you there?"

"No."

"Why can't you leave?"

"I don't want to. If I do, I'll be alone." The truth was so easy for her to say.

"You don't have to be alone."

"But I am. I always am."

"Do you want someone there with you to help you and keep you safe?"

That sounded so good. Not to be alone. To have someone there to protect her and help her. "Yes."

"You can have a guide, someone to be there with you all the time, someone who can take you to the safe place whenever you want to go back there. But you have to make that person, visualize that person. Make your guide whoever you want, someone who makes you feel the safest. A fairy godmother, a minister, your mother or father, a friend. You imagine the person and let him or her be with you."

Before he finished speaking, she sensed someone there with her by her side in the sun, but she didn't look at the person. She just knew she wasn't alone. The guide was near her, but didn't touch her. Yet there was a closeness that she could literally feel, a oneness that banished her loneliness. The guide didn't speak out loud, but in some way she heard him speak.

Him? Yes, a man with a voice that was as smooth and gentle as honey. And it was inside her. "You're going to be all right. You're safe," the guide said over and over again in her mind. "Trust me."

Chapter 8

And at the same time, R.J.'s voice was overlaying the guide's voice in her.

"Lyndsey?" R.J. was saying. "Do you have a guide with you now?"

"Yes. I can't see him, but—"

"No, don't tell me about your guide, just use the presence for yourself. It's all yours."

Yes, that's exactly what she wanted.

"Now, do you want to watch what's going to happen, or do you want to be in the picture?" he asked.

She almost said she wanted to be in the picture as long as the guide was with her, but she stopped. "Watch," she breathed.

"When you're ready we'll go back to last Friday, to the afternoon, as you leave work. Can you see yourself?"

She did almost instantly. "Yes." The breeze off the Sound was touching her, the car was ahead in the parking lot. And the guide was there, always there, the soft voice in her mind letting her know she wasn't alone as she watched what was happening.

"What's going on?" R.J. asked.

"I'm . . . walking to the car to go to the bank."

She was there, touching the handle, opening the door, getting inside.

"Skip further ahead when you're at the bank. What are you doing there?"

She was in the bank, standing in line. "Cashing my check."

"Then what?"

"Going outside. The sidewalk's busy. I'm not looking. I'm bumped and my glasses fall. I pick them up. I walk away."

"Who bumped you?"

"I don't know," she said. "I can't see."

"All right, drive to your apartment. As you go, tell me everything you see, everything you notice."

His words made it happen, and she was driving toward the parking structure. "Sunny . . . really clear . . . nice."

"Lots of people around?"

She watched the picture. "Now? No. It's later than usual. I didn't go right home. No one's there. The doors open and I drive in."

"What does it look like now?"

"Cool, soft light, cars parked."

"Any people?"

"No, I don't think so."

"Look carefully. Is there anything out of the ordinary?"

She could see it all. Everything exactly the same. "No."

"Keep driving."

"Safe, you're safe," the guide was whispering all the time, a chant, a reassurance, a guarantee. "You're safe."

She saw herself driving, going forward, toward her spot, then pulling into it. Without warning she was in the car, she was touching the handle to the door, she was getting out. And the guide's words were still there, over and over again. And she let them encompass her, even when the action kept going. She was getting out, her feet hitting the concrete, the cool air on her arms and face.

The horror was there, but it was held back, stopped in some way, yet it was all around her, raw and alive, but not touching her because of the soft whispers of the guide. She reached for her purse in the car, then felt the hand on her arm.

Everything changed. The whispers were gone, and Lyndsey suddenly knew she was going to die. She held up her hands as she jerked back, trying to escape. And she screamed in her mind for her guide to help. Then he did. She could feel herself being pulled away from the killer by a force that was stronger than the evil waiting for her. She looked back, seeing only shadows, but in that moment she understood something. But before she could figure out exactly what it was, she was swept clear of the shadows and the threat there. The guide was with her, taking her away from danger.

"I won't let anything hurt you," the guide's voice was whispering to her, the words echoing inside her. "Come back to the safe place." And she could feel the guide willing her back to safety and peace.

She easily drifted back to the ocean and water and peace and safety. She almost cried with relief as she basked in the comfort she found there. "You're safe," the guide's voice was saying. "I'm here to make sure you're not hurt." Then his voice began to grow softer and softer. "I promised you. You're safe. You're safe. You're safe."

Then it was mingling with R.J.'s voice. "Are you in the safe place?"

"Yes," she murmured.

"Are you all right?"

"Yes."

"It's time to bring you back. I'll count backward from five, and you can open your eyes whenever you want to."

As he counted back, Lyndsey reluctantly let go of the safe place.

"Four."

She moved inexorably toward reality, and she couldn't shake a sadness at leaving the guide behind.

"Three."

She wanted to hear the words that had seemed to fill her when the guide was there.

"Two."

She craved that sense of everything being in order and right.

"One," R.J. said softly, and the safe place was gone.

Lyndsey could feel her fingers lying on the soft fabric of the reclining chair. She inhaled and exhaled, then slowly opened her eyes. She felt dampness on her cheeks, moisture on her lashes, and realized she'd been crying. But why? Was it from the fear that had been about to engulf her? Was it from the sadness of leaving the safe place?

She didn't know. No more than she knew what she'd almost remembered. The thing she'd lost when the guide had pulled her away.

"Lyndsey?" R.J. said.

"Mmm?"

"Did you remember anything?"

"I don't know. I thought . . ." She swiped at her face, feeling the moisture on her cheeks. "There was something, but it was gone before I knew what it was."

"Did you see anything about the killer?"

"No. He wouldn't let me."

"Who wouldn't?"

"The guide. He was there, sort of willing me away from it. I should have looked. I should have made myself stay."

"No, he's there to make sure you're not hurt." She was quiet, knowing R.J. was right. "Lyndsey. What are you thinking about?" R.J. asked.

She exhaled, then opened her eyes to the gently lit room, but she didn't look at R.J.. "That I should have looked," she whispered.

"You will, maybe the next time."

"I'm sorry it wasn't this time," she murmured, but she was wondering if the kiss had triggered all of this. No, it was more than that. It was a basic need in her for a man like this in her life. A basic need that would never be filled. She knew without having to think it over that there was only one R.J. in this world, and another woman had had all of his love.

"That's all right. Maybe you can break through. You're very close."

"Yes, so close," she murmured, knowing how close she was to a lot of things. Since Friday, her life had changed so much that she barely recognized herself.

The door clicked open, and she heard the police officer who was stationed by the door say, "Dr. Tyler, Detective MacClain sent me in here to stay with the lady while you go and talk to him."

"What's going on?" R.J. asked as he stood.

"I don't know. He just said to stay here until you come back, or until he does."

Lyndsey slipped on her glasses and looked up at R.J. as he turned to her. "Stay here. I'll be right back."

She watched him leave, then she pushed down the footrest and sat up. "Why did they send you in here?" she asked the policeman.

He shrugged and leaned against the door. "I don't really know, ma'am, but I've got orders to stay put."

Lyndsey felt the chill of the cold tile under her bare feet. "Can I go into my own room to get some slippers?" she asked, pointing to the adjoining door.

He stood straight. "I don't see why not. I'll come with you."

"That's not necessary. I'll be right back."

"All right," he said, leaning back against the door, crossing his arms on his chest.

"Thanks." She crossed to the door and went into her room, closing the door after her. It seemed overly bright after the dimness, and she took just a moment to let her eyes adjust, then she moved to the bed to get her slippers. And spotted the phone.

They knew who she called, where she called, and when she called. And she didn't care right now. She picked up the receiver, put through the long distance call and heard it ring twice before the answering machine came on. Rob's voice repeated the same message she'd heard the first time. She hung up, and knew who she had to call.

She pushed the long distance number, heard it ring three times on the other end, before a woman answered.

"Hello?"

"Estelle?"

"Yes. But I don't know who—?"

"It's Lyndsey Peters," she said in a low voice.

The head of the woman's shelter, Estelle Gray, was silent for a long moment, then said, "Lyndsey, I won't ask where you are, because I don't want to know. What I want to know is how you are."

Estelle had been her only friend and confidante during the months in the shelter after she'd left Rob. And the woman was the one person Lyndsey knew who would understand completely what she was going through. She wanted nothing more than to tell her what had happened, then she decided against it.

She'd drawn Estelle and the people at the shelter into the center of her problems before, but not again. All she needed right now was some answers. "I'm doing fine," she replied. "I'm settling in."

"Good. You deserve a new life."

Lyndsey closed her eyes. Some new life. "I just wanted to check and find out if Rob was still bothering you?"

"I told you not to worry about what goes on here."

"Estelle, I need to know. Has he been coming by trying to find me?"

"Yes. He was outside the shelter for days, just watching, waiting. We were thinking of calling the police."

"Is he still coming by?"

"Lyndsey, that's not your problem anymore."

"I know, but—"

"He was here a week or so ago. I told him I didn't know where you were, and if I did, I would never tell him. I basically told him to get lost, then had him shown out and told not to come back or he'd deal with the police."

"Did he come back?"

"No, and that surprised me. I thought he'd keep it up, the way he had before, until we had to take action."

If Rob was in Dallas, Lyndsey knew he would have kept it up. She opened her eyes to the quiet room. Unless he'd left the city. "Estelle, I don't know how I can ever thank you for what you've done for me, all of you at the shelter."

"That's why we're here, Lyndsey. And you made the right choice. You know that, don't you?"

"Yes, I do, and I'm sorry Rob caused so much trouble for everyone."

"No apologies necessary. He's the one doing it, not you. Now, tell me what you're up to."

"I've got a job." She didn't let herself think that the job was probably long gone by now. One more thing Rob had cost her, but she'd get another one, and another one, until Rob was gone and she could stay in one place forever.

She heard the policeman in the other room moving around. "I...I have to go, but I wanted to...to keep in touch."

"Lyndsey, I'll understand if you don't call again."

Estelle understood everything, even the fact that Lyndsey wouldn't be calling again. "Goodbye," she said and hung up.

She had barely put the receiver back in place when the young policeman looked into the room. "I don't have any slippers," she said quickly.

"Ma'am, they're under the bed," the man said.

"Oh, thanks," she said, stooping to get them. She pushed her feet into the slippers and spotted the newspaper R.J. had thrown away. She bent to take it out of the trash, then got on the bed. "I'll just stay in here and read," she said to the policeman. "Is that all right?"

He glanced around the room, then nodded. "Sure. I'll stay in here with you." He crossed to the corridor door and leaned against it facing her.

Lyndsey looked down at the paper, this time reading each article on the murders. R.J. had been right, the police gave out very few real details. She was a nebulous "unnamed victim" who had survived but was in a very deep coma. There was speculation about everything, not just about rape, and Lyndsey realized that she knew little more after reading the articles than she did before.

She put down the paper, leaned back against the coolness of the headboard and waited for R.J. to come back.

R.J. spotted Russ just beyond the elevators near the pay phones talking to one of the uniformed policemen. The two men were deep in conversation as R.J. got closer, and he heard Russ saying, "Keep this under your hat."

"Yes, sir."

Russ glanced at R.J., hesitated, then spoke to the officer. "You stay here and keep a close watch until the lab boys get here."

The officer nodded. "Yes, sir."

"What's going on?" R.J. asked.

Russ looked at him and spoke in a low voice. "He's been here again." He pointed to the nearest phone on the phone bank. "There. They found them a few minutes ago. Thank God, one of men was smart enough to know what he found when he was calling in."

R.J. stared at the tiny balls of foil someone had discarded on the shelf under the phone. "Are you sure they're the same?"

"In my gut? Yes. Absolutely? No. The lab's going to have to run tests on them, and I'm calling in for forensics to do prints on the phone and this whole area."

The implication of Russ's statement made R.J.'s mouth go dry. "He's been here again," he said, echoing Russ's first words, his voice so tight he barely recognized it.

Russ nodded, "It looks that way."

All R.J. could think of was the man had been out in the open, within shouting distance of Lyndsey's room. This wasn't loitering in the stairwell. "What are you going to do?"

Russ glanced at the uniformed officer. "Let me know when everyone arrives. I'll be in Dr. Tyler's room."

The man nodded, then Russ began to walk down the hallway. R.J. fell in step beside him. "Don't look so grim," he said as he slanted R.J. a look. "I've got a plan."

"What sort of plan?"

Russ tugged at the cuffs of his rumpled coat. "We've got a man at the front doors, a man at the elevators, outside Lyndsey's room and at all the access points to this floor. The nurse is one of ours. I thought we were covered as long as the killer thought Lyndsey was in a coma."

"You were damned wrong," R.J. muttered, feeling a fear deep in his soul that he could barely endure.

"I miscalculated. And I'm making it right." Russ looked up and down the corridor. "We're closing down this section of the floor completely. Checks at the elevators and stairs. All incoming people will have to be cleared. No civilian patients within five rooms of Lyndsey and no civilian personnel in the area."

"That's your plan?"

Russ kept walking with R.J. beside him. "Not completely. We know the idea that she's here will bring him back. We're going to set up a dummy room and draw him there. Maybe we'll get lucky."

"Lyndsey survived one attack by this madman. That was luck. She won't survive another attack. I don't even know if she can survive remembering what happened to her the first time. I won't let you do this to her."

"He didn't get to her, R.J., and he's not going to. We just miscalculated."

"Miscalculated?" R.J. said, grabbing Russ by the arm to stop him in front of Lyndsey's room. "He's been within shouting distance twice and you say you miscalculated?"

Russ shrugged, pulling his arm away from R.J.'s hold. "I thought since we gave out the word Lyndsey was in a coma, he'd be lulled into a false sense of security and lay low until he got word about her condition improving or deteriorating. Now we know that he's going to make sure she never comes out of the coma. And he'll play right into our hands if he comes back here. We'll be ready for him the next time."

"And what's Lyndsey, your bait?" he ground out.

The door to Lyndsey's room opened and the young police officer looked out. He saw Russ and R.J. "You had both better come in here."

R.J. went past Russ and brushed by the policeman to get into the room. He didn't know what he expected, but he found Lyndsey standing by the bed, her face tight and drawn. She waited until Russ was in the room and the door was closed before she spoke in a flat voice. "He was here, in the hospital again, wasn't he?"

Before R.J. could say anything, Russ tried to evade the direct question with, "We don't know for sure, but—"

"No," she bit out, hugging herself tightly with her arms. "I know he's been here."

Russ nodded to the policeman by the door, and the young man slipped out into the corridor, closing the door behind him. Then Russ turned back to Lyndsey. "We've got a little problem."

Lyndsey stared at Russ. "You owe me the truth. I'm not some reporter you're trying to string along." She looked at R.J., her eyes filled with an incredible mixture of burning anger and heart-wrenching vulnerability. "This is my life, and I deserve to know what's going on, don't I?"

R.J. went to within a few feet of her, and it unnerved him to see a trembling in her shoulders. The basic fear he felt had to be a hundred-fold worse for her. "Yes, he was here again by the phones in the corridor."

She almost collapsed back against the bed, and she pressed her hand flat on the sheet for support.

"Lyndsey," Russ said quickly. "We don't know this for sure. We won't until we get the lab results back."

Lyndsey never looked at Russ. It was as if she didn't even hear him. Her eyes never left R.J. "I'm leaving."

Russ took a step toward her. "You can't."

She looked at him, her expression tightening more with each passing moment. R.J. could see her stiffen her spine, and he wondered if she'd gotten through the horror of her life with her husband by sheer willpower. "I *can* leave, and I'm going to. He'll be in here next."

"No, he won't."

She looked at R.J. "Will you help me?"

R.J. went closer, letting himself reach out to touch her shoulder. It seemed a poor second to his need to hold her to him, but he didn't move any closer. "Where can you go?"

He felt her take a shaky breath. "I don't know. Anywhere. I just know I won't stay here."

"Lyndsey, the police are all over this floor." Russ spoke quickly. "I've got everything covered."

She turned on Russ. "He'll be back, and I'm getting out of here." She moved away from R.J.'s touch and hurried to the small dresser where the nurse had put the few clothes they'd brought for her. She tugged open the drawers and pulled the clothes out, tossing them onto the top of the dresser.

"You don't have anyplace to go where you'll be safer than here," Russ said.

Lyndsey spun around, some of her clothes clutched to her chest as if they could help protect her in some way. "I'll disappear. I can't help you, anyway. I don't know what the man looks like." She glanced around the room, then crossed to pick up the tote bag the nurse had left by the foot of the bed. She knew how to disappear, and this time she'd do a better job of it. She put the tote on the bed and began to stuff her clothes into it. When she went back to get the rest of the clothes off the dresser, she spoke in a breathless voice. "I'll let you know if I remember anything."

Lyndsey went back, pushed the other clothes in the bag, did up the zipper and put the strap over her shoulder before she turned to look at R.J. He was closer now, not more than a foot from her, and she felt a stab of deep regret that she would never seen him again. "There's nothing you can say that will make me stay here. I'm leaving."

"No, you can't," he said in a low, rough voice. "It's too dangerous. Stay here for a bit and give me a chance to figure out what to do. There has to be a way to protect you and get the killer, too." He wasn't touching her, but she felt as if he was holding her to the spot. "Just give me time to see what can be done. I won't let anything hurt you. Trust me," he said, and the words echoed in her, a repeat of something else.

Then she knew. The guide's voice. The guide was R.J., at least the essence of him, that caring gentleness that she had never known in her life. And she knew why she had been crying when she woke from the session with R.J. It was from the sadness she felt knowing that only in an unreal world of make believe would she experience those feelings. Not here. Not now. And that was one more reason to leave here as quickly as she could. Self-preservation came in many forms.

"I have to go," she said, but with less force.

"I know. But I'm just asking for an hour."

She looked away from the intensity of his hazel eyes and murmured, "All right." She dropped her bag on the floor, climbed on the bed and sat Indian-style in the middle of the mussed sheet. "I'll wait one hour. Then I'm going."

He stared at her hard for a long moment before heading for the door that led to his room. He motioned Russ to follow him, and without another word, the two men left, closing the door behind them.

Lyndsey fell back on the bed, covered her eyes with her forearm and waited.

"Thanks," Russ said as soon as the door was closed. "You saved the day."

"I bought one hour, Russ, that's all. At the end of that hour, you have to come up with something that will convince Lyndsey that she'll be protected and safe from that maniac if he comes back looking for her, or she's out of here."

"I know, I know," Russ muttered as he stood at the foot of the bed, then turned to look at R.J. "That's a big order."

"Can you do it?" R.J. asked.

"I have to. She's the only trump card I've got in this hand."

R.J. moved from the closed door and got close enough to Russ that he didn't have to raise his voice. "Just find a solution or you don't have anything."

"I've got a solution. I just thought of it."

"What is it?"

"What we need is a safe place for Lyndsey where no one will think to look, a place that can be totally cut off and protected from surprise visitors."

"That sounds good. Where is this place?"

"Bob's lodge."

"What?"

Russ didn't blink. "Bob Hanlahan's lodge on Lyon Island."

Lyon Island, the place R.J. had gone to die. A speck of land in Puget Sound, land drenched in green freshness, quietness and clean air, and cut off from the mainland except by a ferry service that ran three times a day. A place where R.J. had spent dark days and darker nights, shutting himself off from the world, from everything that had reminded him of Maddy.

He'd formed a close relationship with numerous bottles of whiskey, existing during days that blended into one another until weeks passed, and losing any sense of time and place. He'd sat on the beach from morning to night, never moving, just being.

"The cabin's perfect for what we need, and Bob's not up there now. I think he'd agree to loaning it out to the department for a goodly sum, and—" he paused for effect "—it's totally isolated."

The cottage was on the far northern tip, double storied, wooden framed, overlooking the Sound with Seattle in the distance. And R.J. remembered rooms of silence and emptiness, rooms that had held his anger and his grief. "It's one idea," he murmured.

Russ shrugged. "It's the best I can come up with, short of locking her up at Central Jail for her own protection."

Russ was right, and R.J. admitted, "She'd be safe there."

"Yes, she would be. As safe as she *can* be until we catch the killer."

"Then take her there and protect her until this is over with," R.J. said.

"Do you think she'll go?"

"I don't know. She's pretty strong-willed."

"Yeah, I noticed," Russ agreed. "But we have one thing working in our favor."

"What's that?"

"She trusts you. If you ask her to go, she'll do it."

R.J. felt a heaviness in his chest, because he was almost certain it was the truth. He'd made Lyndsey trust him, and that was a two-edged sword. The more she trusted him, the more vulnerable she was, and the more vulnerable he seemed to be where she was concerned. "I can talk to her, see if she'll go with your people."

"No, see if she'll go with you."

"Me?"

"Sure. You can't step out now. You're close to finding answers, and, as I said before, she trusts you. Who better to go with her and stay with her?"

R.J. recoiled at the idea. Not from revulsion, but because of what he'd been when he'd been there before, and because of what he understood was happening to him right now. He was getting close to Lyndsey, so close that he knew he was in danger of compromising himself professionally and exposing himself emotionally. Right now he had no idea which fate would be worse than the other.

"Russ, I didn't figure on anything like this." That was the truth. He'd never figured on any woman touching him this way again, or of his being so afraid of what could happen if he let himself care. "I can't do it."

"You have to, R.J., and you know you do." Russ frowned. "You can't fold on me now."

Fold? God, he was barely able to support himself, let alone someone else. The idea was unnerving. When he didn't say anything, Russ went closer to him and asked, "What's going on with you?"

"What do you mean?"

Russ stared at R.J., then his eyes widened and he hit his forehead with the heel of his hand. "Brother, have I been blind."

"Russ, I—"

Russ held up one hand. "It's my fault. I've been so tied up with this case that I didn't see what was going on right under my nose."

"I don't know what you're talking about."

"She got to you, didn't she, R.J.?"

R.J. felt a knot in his stomach. Was it that obvious, the way he had to fight to maintain some semblance of professional behavior around Lyndsey? "You know I get involved in my cases," he hedged, not about to discuss his mixed-up feelings with Russ. "This case isn't any different."

"I'm not talking about a case, R.J., I'm talking about the woman."

R.J. kept himself from touching his tongue to his lips to see if her taste might still linger there. Russ had no idea how on the mark his observation was. Lyndsey Cole was a woman who could make a man want her with abandon, but he couldn't let that happen with him. He said words to Russ that he hoped would give himself a focus on what his relationship with Lyndsey should be. "I'm her psychiatrist. She's a patient."

"And you'll stay on the case?"

If he could hold on to the words he just said to Russ, he knew he could get through this. And he knew right then that he really could help Lyndsey, and this was the first time in a very long time he felt as if he could make a difference. He knew she was close to remembering, and he wanted to be there when it happened. He'd just have to deal with his own jumbled emotions.

"Yes, I will."

"Good, then we'll go ahead with our plans. Give me fifteen minutes before you go back in there and try and convince Lyndsey to go to the island with you."

"Aren't you coming to talk to her with me?"

"No, I've got other things to take care of before she can leave here," Russ said. "I need to contact Bob and make sure we can get the lodge. And it'll have to be clean and stocked. I'll send a couple of detectives with you as bodyguards." Russ looked at his watch. "It's eight now. I have to arrange for a car and a special ferry service, give Bob time to make arrangements. With any luck, we'll get you out of here by midnight."

"That's another question, how do we get her out without being seen?"

"Let me work on that," Russ said.

R.J. crossed to the easy chair and dropped down in it with a sigh. "Let me know if we can do it, then I'll go and talk to Lyndsey."

"I'll get back as soon as I can," Russ said and headed for the door.

Chapter 9

It was five minutes short of the agreed-upon hour when Lyndsey saw R.J. come back through the connecting door. She hadn't moved. She hadn't dared. If she had, she knew she would have taken off and run for dear life. She'd promised them an hour, and she'd wait that long, then she was leaving.

She looked at R.J. as he closed the door and came to the bed. In some way he looked different, maybe tired or nervous, she wasn't sure which, but it showed in the lines etched at either side of his mouth and in the tense way he held his head. He raked his fingers through his thick hair and hesitated, as if searching for the right words to say.

"Russ worked out something," he finally said.

She raised one brow. "And you were chosen to explain it to me?"

His expression tightened perceptibly. "Russ has to get things arranged."

"What's his idea?"

"There's an island in the Sound, a place called Lyon Island. Have you ever heard of it?"

She nervously smoothed the denim on her knees as she shook her head. "No, but I don't really know this area that well."

"It's one of the small islands west of the city in the Sound. It's cut off except for three ferry crossings each day, one early morning, one at noon, and one in the evening. There's a lodge there that's approached by a single road. It's totally defensible." He paused. "Going to the lodge and staying there until this is over is your best chance to survive all of this."

"How did Russ find this lodge?"

"One of the men in the department owns it."

"And he's willing to just hand it over for this?"

"Russ has known Bob, the man who owns it, for years. He loaned it to me, once. And I think it would be perfect."

She wasn't sure where the idea came from, but for a heartbeat all she could think of was that R.J. had used it, and he'd probably been there with his wife. The idea of going to a place where he'd been in love and happy didn't set well with her. She shook her head. "I don't know, I—"

"What don't you know?"

She kept her eyes on her hands. Damn it, she didn't want to feel like this. She didn't want to have all her reason fogged by a response to this man that seemed to come from her soul and engulf her. And to be reticent because he'd been there with his wife, a place where they'd laughed and loved, no, she didn't know how to deal with it.

"Maybe the man's using it himself. Maybe his kids are."

She'd never asked Russ about R.J. having children, but suddenly she wondered if he did, and if they'd been there with him and his wife. The idea brought a deepening of the strange jealousy she'd felt before. She'd wanted children. But when she'd lost the baby she'd become pregnant with during her first year of marriage, she'd almost been grateful. The idea of Rob's child was something she couldn't bear now. And after the miscarriage, she'd made very sure she would never get pregnant again by Rob.

The memory of that time came in waves for her, as overwhelming as anything that was happening to her right now. She touched her tongue to her lips, then looked up at R.J. He'd been talking, and she had no idea what he'd been saying. "I'm sorry, what?"

"He's single. Bob, the guy who owns it, and Russ has already found out he's willing to loan it for this purpose. So, it's there. It's as safe as any place can be until the killer's found. It makes sense for you to go."

"If I go, does Russ go with me?"

He shook his head. "No, he can't. I'll go with you."

That idea shook her even more. Alone with R.J. on an island cut off from the world? It made her chest tighten and breathing become hard. "Who else?"

"You, me and a couple of plainclothes cops. There's a garage with living quarters above it at the top of the road, about a hundred yards from the lodge. They can stay there."

And she'd be alone in a lodge with R.J., in the same lodge he'd probably shared with his wife. "I don't think that'll work."

"Why not?"

"I can't just go off like that," she said, grasping for a reason to go in another direction. "I have a job, and—"

"Russ finally talked with your boss. He's being very cooperative. Says you can take all the time you need. He understands, and he'll keep quiet about it. We can get your work for you and bring it to the lodge, if it goes on very long."

"My contacts. I need to get them tomorrow."

He reached in his pocket and took out two small plastic vials. "Here you go."

She stared at them. "How . . . ?"

"Russ got them."

"But it's Sunday, and the doctor—"

"The doctor was very cooperative with the police." He frowned. "Is there anything else?"

She looked at R.J., admitting to herself that she'd been caught throwing up false barriers. She took the vials, then asked a question she needed an answer to. "Do you think I should do this?"

His eyes narrowed. "I think it can work."

"That's not what I asked you. Would you do it, if you were me?"

"Russ is good at what he does," R.J. said, moving away from her to drop down in the chair. He looked back at her as he rested his elbows on the arms and laced his fingers loosely on his stomach. "He thinks it can work."

She hesitated, then slid off the bed and stood in front of R.J., the vials containing the contacts in either hand. "Would you do it or would you let someone you cared about do it?"

For a reason she didn't understand, that question seemed to strike R.J. hard. He narrowed his eyes as if he didn't want to look at her directly, and he didn't speak for a long moment while he seemed to be staring at his hands. Then he inhaled harshly and looked up at her. "Yes, I would. I think it's the only chance you have."

"If we go there, what then?"

"We keep trying to get you to remember."

"And if I don't go?"

R.J. stood abruptly, almost bumping into Lyndsey, and she had to back up to keep from making the contact. He looked down at her, toe-to-toe. "Honestly?"

"Yes."

"If you don't, Russ will have you locked up for your own protection in the downtown jail."

"Then I don't have a choice, do I?"

"I'm afraid not."

She turned from him, bumping his arm with hers and feeling awareness shoot through her whole being. Quickly she moved away from him to the foot of the bed. She had the horrible sensation of being out of control again, and she hated it, that feeling of having no choice in her own fate. She put the vials with the contacts on the bed, picked up her tote bag and put it on the bed. She fingered the zipper hasp, and without looking at R.J., she asked, "How can we get out of here without anyone seeing?"

"Russ is working it all out, and the doctor's coming back in for one more check before he agrees to let you go."

She glanced at R.J., at a man of planes and angles, darks and lights. A man who, if she was honest with herself, gave her the courage to do what she knew she had to do. "If I pass the physical, when do we leave?"

"As soon as Russ has everything in place."

* * *

When Lyndsey left her room at midnight, she was in a wheelchair wearing her terry-cloth bathrobe, with her glasses safely tucked in her bag and her contacts in. A gray blanket covered her legs and feet, hiding her sneakers and jeans, and most of her hair and forehead was hidden by fresh bandages. R.J. wore a doctor's coat, a stethoscope dangled by the earpieces from his neck, and he pushed the wheelchair.

Lyndsey looked around as they entered the hallway, seeing police stationed by the elevators, a door marked Stairs, and her own door. The policeman closest to them looked at R.J., gave a thumbs-up sign, then motioned to the elevators. "It's clear," he said. "Take the first elevator. No one will bother you on it. They'll meet you at the bottom."

"Thanks," R.J. said, then pushed the chair down the tiled hallway and stopped by the first elevator. The policeman there was holding the door open for them, and R.J. pushed Lyndsey into the car and turned the chair so Lyndsey faced the doors. The young policeman looked at Lyndsey. "Best of luck to you," he said, and let go of the doors to let them shut.

As the elevator started down, R.J. spoke in a low voice, as if he was afraid of being overheard. "When we get to the first floor, we'll come out in the lobby area, then go to the right, back to the Emergency Area. That's where we'll get the ambulance."

"Why didn't we go out a back way?" she asked, her hands clutched so tightly under the blanket that they ached. "I feel like we're walking into the lion's den going out to the lobby."

"Russ thinks this will throw the press off. They're watching all the exits we could be sneaking out of, and they're keeping a close eye on your doctor. Who, by the way, even as we go down in this car, is telling the press there's no change in your condition. So all we have to do is act as if we know what we're doing and get to the ambulance.''

Right then, the elevator came to a soft stop, and the doors slid open. Lyndsey could hear a commotion coming from the left, and jumped when R.J. touched her on the shoulder. "Here we go," he whispered, then the contact was gone and Lyndsey was being pushed out into the lobby.

For a second she panicked at being so exposed, but she realized no one was paying any attention to her and R.J. Everyone seemed to be heading toward the front of the hospital.

As R.J. pushed her in the opposite direction, she could hear voices raised, drowning out the mood music coming over the speakers. They went down the corridor, passing just a scattering of doctors and nurses, turned a corner, kept going to another corridor. A lighted sign ahead of them read Emergency Services, and that's where R.J. pushed the wheelchair through double doors into a short corridor.

"Almost there," R.J. said, and Lyndsey looked ahead at the end of the hallway where a doctor was opening another set of doors for them. R.J. pushed her through, and they were outside on a raised ramp area protected by a heavy overhang. Straight ahead, backed up to the ramp, was an ambulance with its back doors open.

Before she could say or do anything, the wheelchair stopped and R.J. was in front of her. "This is it," he said, then unexpectedly reached down and, in one smooth movement, took the blanket off her and was lifting her out of the chair.

Her shock at his actions wasn't any greater than the shock at herself when she wrapped her arms around his neck and held him as he carried her to the ambulance. She closed her eyes, bombarded by the scent and essence of R. J. Tyler. She was surrounded by heat and safety, and she had a sudden, crystal-clear memory of the guide when she'd been hypnotized. This was part of the essence of R.J. that she had put in that guide.

She felt R.J. walking, then duck, and she was being lowered and set on something firm and cool. She opened her eyes to find that she was sitting on a pallet on the floor in the back of the ambulance, and R.J. was moving across from her. Then the doors were swung shut, a siren started up, its shrill noise so loud that she wanted to cover her ears, and they were moving. Only a low light was on in the back of the ambulance.

R.J. sat facing her, leaning back on a stainless-steel cabinet, his white coat discarded beside him. He smiled, a fleeting expression that barely touched his shadowy eyes. "You'd better brace yourself. This could be a rough ride."

She shrugged out of the bathrobe, then tugged her shirt down and smoothed it before she scooted back to lean against the opposite wall. She looked at R.J. as he tugged the stethoscope off and laid it on the coat beside him. Then he glanced up at Lyndsey, his features softly blurred by the low light.

"So far, so good. When we get to the ferry landing, we have to leave the ambulance as quickly as possible and get on the ferry. Russ will have a car for us on the ferry, and the two plainclothesmen will be there."

Lyndsey tugged at the bandages on her face and head, freeing herself from the thin gauze. As she wadded them up in her hand, she stared down at them. "It looks like the disguise worked," she said over the scream of the siren.

"People see what they think they see," R.J. said.

She dropped the bandages on the floor, then bent her legs and wrapped her arms around them. She rested her chin on her knees. "Yes, they sure do." How else could anyone explain people perceiving Rob as a devoted husband and good man? They saw what he wanted them to see, what they expected to see. The siren echoed all around, and the ambulance rounded a corner so sharply that Lyndsey had to brace herself. And a memory that had flashed into her mind just hours ago came back to her. Without thinking, she spoke out loud. "I hate ambulances."

"You've been in one before?"

She looked up at R.J., thankful for the shadows that seemed to be a buffer between herself and this man. "I was in one once," she admitted, then rested her forehead on her knees and closed her eyes.

"Was it anything serious?" R.J. asked, his voice overly loud when the sirens stopped abruptly.

She didn't look up. There wasn't any reason to lie to R.J. about that night. And she didn't need painkillers to make her feel free enough to tell him. "It was serious." The words just came. "I lost a baby." Before he could say anything, she said, "It was Rob's fault. There'd been an argument. I don't even remember what started it now, but it got out of hand pretty fast." She opened her eyes, but didn't look up. She kept her forehead pressed to her knees, in some way not feeling so exposed as she talked.

"Rob had hit me before, but just a few times. He promised that he would never do it again. He even cried once." She bit her lip. "Anyway, I tried to get away from him. But I wasn't fast enough, and I stumbled, and he caught me by the arm. When I jerked away, I fell backward and down the porch steps at the back of the house."

She took a shuddering breath and closed her eyes. "I regained consciousness in the ambulance on the way to the hospital, and I could smell the engine fumes and the odor of medicine all mixed up together. And Rob was riding beside me . . . crying.

"Everyone was so worried about him." She laughed, a short bitter sound. "Poor man, I was clumsy. I fell because I wasn't paying attention, and I'd lost the baby my husband obviously wanted so desperately."

"A baby?" R.J. asked softly.

The anger that had always been there, mixed with bitterness that had always threatened to suffocate her when the memory came, seemed to diminish just from the act of telling this man about that night. "The baby was gone before it really was there. The nurses were so impressed by my husband, who stayed with me every minute from the time I fell until I was in the hospital asleep from painkillers. Then he stayed with me until I was able to come home."

"You don't have to tell me this," he said.

But she did. Once she'd started, she had to finish. "He didn't want that baby. He was glad it was gone." She closed her eyes so tightly that she saw colors explode behind her lids. "He was afraid I'd say something, that everyone who thought he was a saint would hate him."

"You wanted the baby?"

She exhaled in a rush. "More than anything. But when it was gone, I didn't want any more. Not after that. No more than I ever want to be in a relationship like that again." She was shocked that her lashes were damp, but there were no real tears. "I trusted Rob. I thought I loved him. I was wrong, so wrong. Never again."

R.J. touched her hand, and her head shot up. She hadn't even heard him move close to her, and when she looked up he was on his knees in front of her. His strong hand was on hers, but it wasn't a strength that she feared.

"Lyndsey, that's all over. One bad experience can't define your whole life. You have to let go of it and get on with your life."

She sat very still, not sure if she wanted his touch to stay on her, or if she wanted to draw back from it. "Let go? Emotionally I let go of Rob a very long time ago. Physically I let go when I walked out. That's what I was doing moving here. He just won't let go of me."

The ambulance turned another corner sharply, and Lyndsey couldn't stop sliding sideways into R.J. For a split second, she wanted to put her arms around him and hold on to him, and never let him go. Then she faced reality and scooted back against the wall.

"Is that what you want?"

"Of course. Why wouldn't I want that?"

"Why did you call him?"

That brought her up short, and she rested her head back against the wall of the ambulance. She could feel the vibration of the tires on the road in the metal. "I don't know," she murmured. "It was an impulse."

"It could have given him the idea that you wanted to contact him, that you regretted your break from him."

She felt sickness in her middle. "That's the last thing I want." She looked at R.J., a thought coming that really scared her. "Russ wouldn't contact Rob, would he?"

"I doubt it. He has never mentioned doing it."

"If he does..." She bit her lip hard. "I should have said something, but I forgot. Damn it. With everything else, I didn't think about it until now."

"Hey, even if he does, Rob can't get to you."

She looked at R.J. "Yes, he could. That's why I left Dallas. That's why I'm here, and why I'm in this mess. He can't know where I am."

"All right. I'll talk to Russ. I'll make sure he doesn't give anything away."

"Thank you," Lyndsey breathed, then rested her forehead back on her knees again. "I should have thought about it earlier. I can't believe I didn't."

"Quit blaming yourself. You're doing fine. You almost remembered what happened during our last session, and soon this will all be over. Then you can get on with living."

Living? She couldn't begin to imagine what living would be after this was over and done. All she knew for sure was there wouldn't be an R. J. Tyler in that life. "It isn't that simple," she whispered.

"No, it isn't. But it won't be as hard as you think it might be. You've got choices to make."

"I make lousy choices."

"No, just reactive choices. You were looking for one thing, and found another. Everyone does that in their lives."

"I was looking for love, and I thought I was in love. But I wasn't."

"Maybe you were and your husband killed it. It takes two people to love. One-sided love is infatuation, not love. Love is give and take, mingling, becoming 'one' as the saying goes. And it takes two. Rob was damaged. He couldn't give you love. It wasn't in him to love anyone, not even himself."

He was right. Rob hadn't known the meaning of love. But R.J. did. He had had the give and take. He'd loved and been loved. And he still loved, even after death. She hugged her legs tightly and looked out the windows at the city at night. "How far is the ferry landing?"

R.J. looked outside. "We're almost there."

Lyndsey looked back at R.J. "Is it all right, I mean, you going to the lodge?"

He looked blank. "Why wouldn't it be?"

"I thought your wife and you must have been there."

He exhaled and shrugged. "Maddy? No. She was never there. I went there after she'd died. Bob offered it to me, and I took him up on it." He looked away from her. "It's isolated, and if you want to be alone, totally alone, it's the place to be." He looked back at her with shadowed eyes in the dimness. "I didn't think I'd ever come back. It just goes to show you you never know what life holds for you."

That was more true than R.J. knew. She would have never guessed she'd be here with this gentle man wondering what life could have been if she'd met him before Rob, and if he'd met her before there had been a Maddy in his life.

The ambulance slowed then and went down a steep drive to come to a stop. Before Lyndsey could move, the back doors were open and Russ was standing there. "You two made it. Any problems?"

R.J. jumped out, turned and held out a hand to Lyndsey to help her get out. "None." She took his support, curling her fingers around his, and jumped out onto a gravel parking area. The night was cold, with the chill of the ocean in a light breeze that ruffled massive trees just above the docking sight.

This low spot was lit by old-fashioned street lamps that lined the access road and a small parking lot along the shoreline to the right. The docking area itself was formed by massive pilings, and the Sound beyond looked dark and forbidding. At the far side of the dock was the car ferry, a large and cumbersome-looking vessel, outlined by flashing lights and with a car ramp that lay on gravel between massive pilings. On the lower level, two cars were parked on the deck, and on the upper deck were sitting areas and closed compartments.

"There's a Bronco parked at the front of the ferry. The keys are in the ignition. Shields and Magee are in the sedan. Everything's taken care of. Now, get going."

R.J. took Lyndsey by the arm and led the way. Together, they stepped onto the ramp that swayed slightly with the motions of the ferry, then onto the wood-plank deck.

As soon as they were on board, a man came up behind them and picked up a heavy chain that had been lying on the scarred wood underfoot. He pulled it across the opening, hitching it to a massive hook on a post on the other side of the ferry. Then he ran up the stairs to the second level.

R.J. led Lyndsey past the sedan to the Bronco and opened the door for her. She climbed inside while he went around and got in behind the wheel. Settling in the bucket seat, she looked away from R.J.'s dark silhouette and gazed out at the night and the ocean.

The sky was overcast with only a few stars breaking through a growing cloud cover. And the Sound was dark and vast all around. The ferry's engines started with a shudder, then a low drone filled the night as the vessel began to inch out of the piling channel.

"How long will it take to get to the island?" Lyndsey asked, her voice echoing strangely in the confines of the car.

"Ten minutes. Maybe a little more. I've never crossed at night. The ferries usually run in the early morning when it's foggy and still, or at noon, or near dusk in the evening."

She settled back in the softness of the seat and was aware of R.J. shifting, moving to sit sideways and rest one hand on the top of the steering wheel. "How did Russ arrange this ferry?"

"You can get anything if you're a cop or if you have money. I suspect that Russ used both to get this trip."

"He's got money?"

"No, but he's one of the best at getting the department to cough up money for special cases, like using Bob's lodge."

"So, I'm a special case?"

"Lady, you're pure gold to the cops. And to the press."

She shifted to look at R.J.'s profile in the darkness. "Did Dr. Levin really lie to the press?"

"He offered. He's tired of them camping out in the lobby, and he's willing to do anything to stop the killer before he strangles another woman."

She unconsciously lifted her hand to her throat, her fingers toying with the collar that covered her bruises. "He's a good man," she breathed.

"Yes, he is," R.J. said.

The ferry began to slow, and Lyndsey lowered her hand to her thigh as she looked at the looming shape of Lyon Island dead ahead. The engines lurched, grinding into reverse, and as the island came closer, Lyndsey could make out little beyond a massive dark silhouette fringed with huge trees on the high ridges above the beach.

"We'll drive off first," R.J. said as he started the engine of the Bronco. "The other car can follow us."

The ferry came to a surprisingly smooth stop in a channel of pilings with a soft bump against the cushion of wood, then it stilled. As R.J. flipped on the headlights of the Bronco, Lyndsey saw the beam cut through the night to expose a heavy chain across the other opening for the ferry. The ramp was being lowered beyond the chain, and there was a level gravel area ahead for the disembarking.

A man came from the right, unhooked the chain, then waved R.J. to go ahead. R.J. drove the Bronco slowly over the chain lying on the deck, down the ramp and onto Lyon Island.

The landing site was little more than a parking lot to the right, some small, boarded-up buildings to the left, and a narrow road that led inland. They drove across the gravel onto the road, then to a Y that went north or south. R.J. drove to the north.

Lyndsey looked out the windows, barely able to make out patches of sky through the canopied branches of the massive trees on either side of the climbing roadway. The headlights barely touched the deep darkness that was all around. Lyndsey felt isolated, cut off from everything she knew, until R.J. spoke and she immediately felt centered.

"It's just four miles north of here," he said.

"Is this a resort area?"

"No, not really. There are islanders who live here all year round. Then there are people who come just for the peace and the fishing."

"There's good fishing around here?"

"The best, and there's nothing like it. You go out in the early morning with the mists coming in off the Sound, the breeze cool and clean. Sitting in a boat all alone, letting the swells of the waves lift you up and down. A person can get lost in it, maybe so lost they never want to come back."

She understood the feeling. That was just what she'd experienced under hypnosis. If she could have, she would have stayed with the guide by the ocean forever. She took a quick breath as they rounded a curve, and for a fleeting moment she had a glimpse of the water below, dark and serene. And she felt almost as if she was duplicating her "safe place" right here.

R.J. was here, the water was all around, but she wasn't at peace. She wondered if she would ever find peace again. Or maybe if she'd found it once, and never would again.

"Here we are," R.J. said, swinging the Bronco off the main road and onto a narrow drive that seemed to climb straight up through a tunnel of trees that grew together overhead.

"Where is 'here'?" she asked, aware of lights behind them cutting through the night.

"The lodge is just at the top of the drive after we pass the gates and the garage." They drove upward, passing pillars on either side that supported heavy wooden gates that stood open. Then they broke into a wide, meadow-like clearing. To the right was the garage, a two-story structure with a steep roof and dormer windows that spilled light onto a wooden-tile roof. Wide double doors on the bottom level gave access for cars and trucks.

Just beyond the garage, a side path broke off from the drive and headed out of sight into thick trees on the far side of the clearing. The drive went straight ahead, and Lyndsey could see the lodge at the end of it.

It was much larger than Lyndsey had thought it would be, with a steep roof, a massive stone chimney that had smoke curling out of it, and a wraparound porch sheltering multipaned windows that were aglow with light. They drove along the front of the house and stopped at the bottom of a sweep of steps that led up to the porch and the entry to the lodge.

The lights from the sedan behind them swept across the house as it pulled into the garage behind them. "I'll go and check with Shields and Magee. Why don't you go on inside, and I'll be right back to bring in the bags?"

Lyndsey got out into crisp night air, and the chill off the water drifted on the breeze that brushed her skin. She looked up at a sky filled with rolling clouds, then she turned to close the car door. Just as she touched the cold metal, she looked at R.J., shadowed in the interior, and she almost said to hurry back, not to leave her too long. But she cut off the words before they became reality. The fact was, she was alone. And she'd be alone when this was over, when R. J. Tyler was out of her life.

She turned and hurried to the steps, taking them two at a time, feeling as if she was running away from something rather than to something. The porch creaked slightly when she stepped onto it and crossed it. She pulled the screen door back and reached for the handle of the solid oak front door. Turning it, she felt the latch click, then the door swung silently back.

Lyndsey stepped into an entry area with a wooden stairway that led up to the second level, directly ahead. An open arch to the right showed a softly lit room dominated by a massive stone fireplace with a chimney that soared up both stories and through the open beamed ceiling. In front of the hearth, a leather couch and two chairs were grouped in a half circle on a creamy fur rug. At the front windows stood a brass spyglass pointed toward the view and sitting on an intricately carved wooden tripod that held it three feet above the floor.

The light in the living room barely touched the room on the left, but Lyndsey could make out a low ceiling over a heavy wooden table and four chairs positioned near the front windows for a view of the Sound at dawn or sunset. Warmth from the fire in the hearth mingled with a faint mustiness; overall was a sweet fragrance of burning wood.

Through the windows on either side of the fireplace, Lyndsey could see the Bronco driving slowly back to the house from the garage. She stepped toward the fireplace to get closer to the heat, but as she passed the spyglass, she heard someone moving behind her. No one was supposed to be here, and R.J. was still outside.

Instinctively Lyndsey reached for the first weapon she could find—the spyglass. In the next second, she was gripping the cold brass like she would have a baseball bat, then, screaming at the top of her lungs for R.J., she spun around to strike out at the man coming up behind her.

Chapter 10

"Hey, lady, hold on!" A bearded man stood not more than three feet from Lyndsey with both hands raised, but not to strike Lyndsey. Instead, he was shielding his head. "Don't hit me."

Lyndsey stood with the spyglass up, ready to swing. She stared at the man, and she knew he wasn't the one who was after her. He certainly wasn't Rob, and she knew in that instant, the man who had tried to kill her had been large, much larger than this man. He was short, not more than five and a half feet tall, with a full beard, short cropped gray hair and dressed in faded jeans along with a plaid wool jacket.

Lyndsey faltered, unsure what to do, then R.J. burst into the house. "Lyndsey, what's wrong?" he demanded, then stopped as he came into the living room and saw the scene in front of him.

"He . . . he came up behind me," Lyndsey gasped.

"First," R.J. said, coming toward Lyndsey, "put the spyglass down. Gently. Just put it down."

Lyndsey looked up at the spyglass she was still holding like a club ready to swing, and she slowly lowered it. "I'm sorry. This was all there was, and I . . ." She stared at the brass telescope. "I thought I could hit him. I didn't know what else to do."

R.J. came to her, taking the spyglass from her hands and turning to put it back on the stand. "Next time try something a little less expensive." He turned to her. "And this poor man is Mel Daniels, the local handyman and Bob's neighbor."

Lyndsey looked back at the man, feeling very foolish. "I'm sorry," she said. "I thought you were someone else."

The man shook his head. "Heaven help you, Dr. Tyler, if she was expecting you."

R.J. laughed at that, a genuine burst of humor that Lyndsey felt echo deep inside her. And for the first time in a very long time, she felt laughter bubbling up in her, and it was a pleasant feeling. "I'll be careful who I take a swing at from now on," she said, then turned to touch the spyglass that had been restored to its former place. "At least I have good taste in weapons. This is beautiful."

"Very," R.J. said, but when Lyndsey looked at him, he wasn't looking at the spyglass. After a moment, his gaze moved to the room. "And this is home for the next few days."

"Bob told me you're here for a little fishing," Mel said as he buttoned his jacket. "Glad to see you're getting back to normal. I stocked the kitchen with food, put up some wood and laid out the beds." He looked from

Lyndsey to R.J. and smiled. "Even fixed the place over the garage like he asked for."

"That's great, Mel. I appreciate your coming out on such short notice."

"No problem," the man said. "Will you be wanting the boat brought down in the morning?"

"Just take it to the beach, and we'll get down to it when we can," R.J. said as he walked the man to the front door.

Lyndsey watched the older man leave, then R.J. followed, and instinctively Lyndsey took a step forward to go after him. She didn't want to be alone. But before she could go any farther, R.J. was back with her tote bag and a brown suitcase. "I dropped these when I heard you scream." A smile twitched at the corners of his mouth. "You almost scared old Mel to death."

"Then we're even," Lyndsey said. "He came sneaking up on me, and I thought..." All of her humor was gone as suddenly as it had come. "He should have said something."

R.J. put the bags down at the foot of the staircase. "Next time he'll whistle 'Dixie' before he comes within a hundred feet of you." He looked across the room at her. "Are you hungry?"

"No, not really. Just tired."

"Then we'll get you settled."

When he started up the stairs, Lyndsey hurried after him, having to take the steps two at a time to keep up. She stepped out into a loft that was positioned above the dining area and with an open wall that looked down over the living room.

Two double beds with wooden frames were against the back wall and covered by heavy beige comforters with a bank of loose pillows against the headboards. A single dresser was on the side wall, and the front wall held four deep dormers with window seats in them. They would be perfect places to view the Sound.

Then Lyndsey looked back at the beds, separated by not more than three feet. She felt her mouth go a bit dry when she realized how close R.J. would be to her while they slept.

"Is there another bedroom?"

"No, this is it." He put her tote on the closest bed and motioned to a side door by the dresser. "Bathroom's in there. Freshen up and get into bed. You look exhausted, and I promised the doctor you'd take it easy."

"I am tired," she admitted, walking past R.J. and wishing he didn't have such a distinctive essence that seemed to fill her with each breath she inhaled. She moved quickly to pick up her bag and head for the bathroom, but she stopped at the door and turned back to R.J. "I won't be long. Then you can get in here."

He shook his head. "Don't worry about me. There's a half bath downstairs off the kitchen. I can get a quick shower there. So take your time."

She hesitated, then turned and went into the bathroom, with its Jacuzzi set low in the floor to the right, a vanity to the left topped with marble, and a clear glass shower stall on the far wall. Towels had been laid out along with toiletries that looked as if they had just been purchased at the store. And they probably have been, she thought as she closed the door and crossed to the vanity.

The wall of mirrors above the sinks reflected back a person she barely recognized. She was so pale without any makeup, but the bruises were more like shadows on her skin than full-blown discolorization and the gash on her temple was almost healed. She undid the buttons on her shirt and stopped as the collar parted. The rope burn was still there, more faded, less raw, but a jolt of reality. She'd almost forgotten about it.

Lyndsey looked away and went to the shower stall to turn on the water. As steam and heat filled the room, she stripped off her clothes, then stepped under the steady stream in the shower. The hot water washed over her, and she stood very still, letting the heat surround her, wishing it could wash away all of the uncertainties and problems she was facing. It couldn't, no more than it could stop her mind from wandering back to thoughts of R.J. and the feeling of being held close to him.

When R.J. heard the water start, he looked at the two beds. Sure he could do this. Sure he could stay professional, and horses could talk. He looked away from the bed and headed for the stairs. He hurried down them and went through the lodge to the back bathroom. In seconds he'd stripped off his clothes and as soon as he heard the upstairs water shut off, he turned on the shower and stepped under the water.

The last time he'd been in here, he'd been so drunk he could barely stand up and Russ had thrown him in, clothes and all, under the cold water. Now he felt alive for the first time since those dark days. That fact shook him to the core. But it was right. And he knew the change had come just days ago when Lyndsey had opened her eyes, when she'd spoken to him, when he'd held her, and when he'd kissed her.

And he knew he was close to being in far too deep to walk away from her. But she didn't want a relationship because of her past, because of all the pain she'd endured. And he didn't want one because he couldn't bear to love and lose again. Yet he wondered if he'd ever be fully alive if he didn't love again?

He couldn't make sense out of his thoughts, so he picked up a washcloth and began to scrub, harder and harder until he felt his skin tingling. But no matter what physical sensations he experienced, the thoughts didn't go away. No more than the image of Lyndsey would leave his mind. No more than the idea of sleeping so close to her in the bedroom loft would stop tormenting him.

He turned off the water, stepped out and reached for a towel. As he dried himself, he heard Lyndsey moving around overhead. Discarding the towel on the vanity, he looked around the room, then realized he hadn't brought his bag in here with him. It was still at the bottom of the stairs.

He reached for the towel again, wrapped it around his hips, swiped at his damp hair to get it off his face, then went out into the kitchen.

Lyndsey pulled on her robe, which Russ must have taken from the ambulance and put into her bag at the ferry landing. Standing in the middle of the bedroom, she tied the belt at her waist and listened. There was no sound at all from downstairs, just the chorus of the night outside. She was alone, and she didn't want to be. Where was R.J.? Would he have gone back to the garage without telling her? She started down the stairs, listening, feeling more and more isolated.

She passed his bag sitting at the foot of the stairs and stepped into the living room. No one was there. She looked at the closed double doors at the back of the room, then hurried over to them, the pile of the animal-skin rug soft under her bare feet. She reached out with both hands and pushed the doors open. In the soft glow of the overhead lights, Lyndsey saw the kitchen, but the white-and-oak room was peripheral to her awareness.

All she seemed to be capable of taking in was R.J. at the sink under a span of windows on the back wall. With both hands pressed flat to the white tile counter, he stood very still, his head bowed. Holding both doors open, she was incapable of doing anything but silently stare. Naked except for an indecently small towel at his hips, with hair curling damply on his neck, R.J. was very still, then he took a deep breath. The action made the muscles ripple in his broad back and his strong shoulders lift. She tried to look away, but found herself staring at his bare, hair-dusted legs and the way his feet were planted on the tiles.

The sight made her mouth go dry and robbed her of the ability to say a thing. But her mind raced. And she suddenly understood first love, when just the sight of the person you loved could turn your mind to mush and make your heart race until it felt as if it could leap right out of your chest.

Love? She couldn't even face the word. Lust, wanting, needing. Those words were bad enough, and they were all accurate. Her body felt as tight as a coiled spring, something deep inside her responding with such furious need that she could barely breathe. Every part of her felt alive, and every part of her felt less than whole. And staring at R.J., she knew that not more than ten feet away from her was the person who just might be able to help her find that lost part of herself. Or, her mind relentlessly finished, she might find something that she couldn't control and would end up destroying her.

As if R.J. sensed her presence, he straightened up, then slowly turned to face her. Lyndsey took a step back out of self-protection, but kept the doors open. In that unguarded moment of obvious surprise at seeing her there, he let his gaze slip over her, taking in her bare feet and shower-dampened hair, then his eyes met hers. For an instant she saw something that only intensified her awareness and made her skin burn.

A teenager? Yes. An embarrassed, awkward teenager who didn't know what to say or what to do. Her only clear thought was of how she'd felt around Rob at the first, knowing it was nothing compared to this, and it had been so wrong. And this was terribly wrong. She had no business feeling like this, and she didn't want to. She could see the awareness in R.J., the heat that could explode, but it wasn't love. The man had loved his wife more than life itself. He'd loved once and loved well. He might need a woman, but she didn't fool herself that she stood a chance at a deeper relationship with the man. Even if she wanted to have that chance.

She pushed the doors back further to click them into place so they'd stay open, then she clutched the lapels of her robe with both hands and pulled them closed. "I didn't hear you down here."

He leaned back against the edge of the counter with his lean hips. "I was looking for my bag."

"It's by the front doors at the bottom of the stairs."

"Yes, I finally remembered that."

She glanced away, trying to look anywhere but at the expanse of tanned skin and brushing of dark hair that took the decided form of a T and trailed down his stomach to the whiteness of the towel. "I was afraid you'd left," she admitted as she glanced around the kitchen.

He took a breath that she could hear, that seemed to echo all around her, and as she looked back at him, he took two steps toward her, his bare feet noiseless on the smooth clay tile. "I promise you, I'll let you know if I leave the house. Actually Russ doesn't want us to go very far."

She let go of the lapels of her robe and pushed her hands into the pockets, clenching them into fists. This man and her reaction to him made her wish she could go a hundred miles in one direction and put that buffer of space between them so she could think clearly and make her body settle down. But she could do that. "I guess I'll be going to bed."

"All right."

She turned from him and stopped, keeping her eyes on the living room through the doors. "Do you have any preference in the beds?"

"No, take your pick."

She nodded and would have made her escape, but R.J. stopped her by saying her name.

"Lyndsey?"

She glanced at him over her shoulder. "Yes?"

"I'll be up later. I'll be down here on the couch for awhile."

She murmured, "Good night," and hurried back upstairs.

R.J. watched her go, then he went for his bag. He took it back into the bathroom, found a pair of jeans and slipped them on. He took out a chambray shirt, but didn't bother putting it on. He just carried it with him into the living room and tossed it over the back of the couch.

He wasn't going upstairs tonight. He knew he couldn't. So he'd sleep on the couch. He walked quietly through the bottom level of the house, checked the doors and windows, then he went back into the living room. At the hearth, he tended to the fire, got it blazing, then went to lie down on the couch. The leather was warmed from the glow of the fire and felt soft under him. But he had real trouble relaxing.

He heard every noise upstairs, every sound, and each one conjured up images that played havoc with his body. It would have been hell to have slept in the other bed. And he knew his decision to stay down here had been the smart one. He rested his forearm over his eyes and tried to relax. But that was easier said than done. His body was tight and uncomfortable, and he tried to reroute his thoughts. But no matter what he did, images of Lyndsey were there. And the taste of her lingered on his tongue.

After half an hour of fighting it, he knew what he had to do. First thing in the morning, he had to call Russ and tell him he couldn't do this any longer. Russ had to take him off the case. Any objectivity he might have possessed at the first was completely gone. This had to end before he did more damage than good to the case and to himself.

The lone man knew something was going on. The movement on the tenth floor was different, less anxious, but as if everyone was waiting for something. Had she come out of the coma or was she dead? He'd wondered about that. If the police might say she was alive just to make him think someone could identify him. Or maybe she was brain dead, but they wouldn't say. Or maybe...

He walked down the corridor away from the nurses' station on the ninth floor of the hospital and knew that it was time to force their hand. He wanted to see for himself, to know what was true and what was a lie. And to put an end to all of this. He had to get into her room.

But he knew he had no chance of getting inside with the guards all around. That had been evident when he'd stood in the stairwell for over an hour last night waiting for a shift change, a lull in the vigil, anything. Then he'd been at the phones, faking a call, watching, waiting. But there had been no glitch, no chink in the armor of her protection.

As he walked down the hall, he took out a stick of gum, stripped it of its foil wrapping and popped it into his mouth. Absentmindedly he rolled the paper into a small ball between his thumb and forefinger, then flicked it into an ash tray at the door of the waiting room.

Get to her. Get to her. Get to her. It chanted in his mind, making his head hurt vaguely. How? he wanted to scream to the heavens. How? Nothing short of the building falling down would make the police on the tenth floor leave their stations. He stopped and stared at a red box on the wall right beside him. The building didn't have to fall down. It just had to look like it was going to burn down.

Fifteen minutes later, when the acrid smoke was seeping from the fire he'd started in the supply closet on the ninth floor and the fire alarm had begun to ring, he was at the stairwell door on the tenth floor. The sprinklers would be set off in the closet by now, but that didn't matter. The smoke was what counted.

He cracked the door open and looked out into the corridor. It was alive with shouts of "Fire!" and "Evacuate!" and he stayed where he was, watching. He watched the young cop outside the door to the room look up and down, then call out to the cops by the elevator. "What's the plan?"

"Fire one floor down. We'll have to evacuate."

That's when he stepped out of the stairwell and jogged down the corridor in the direction of the room. He got to the cop and asked in a breathless voice, "I was sent to help. What do you need?"

The cop shook his head, then shocked the man by saying, "I don't need anything." People were coming from the far ends of the floor, nurses and orderlies with patients in wheelchairs. "You'd better help them," the policeman said, then turned without a backward look at the door to the room he'd been guarding. He broke into a jog, heading for the nurse's station.

This is wrong, all wrong. What about her? he wanted to call after the man. But he kept quiet, moving to one side while people rushed past. A thin haze of smoke was swirling near the ceiling, infiltrating the air system from the floor below. He looked both ways, saw no one was paying any attention to him, then he reached for the door, pushed it open and slipped into the hospital room.

As the door swung shut, he looked at a well-lit, empty room. But it wasn't the emptiness of quick evacuation. It was the emptiness of complete disuse. The bed was made. No medication was around and machines were pushed against the wall and weren't turned on. For a minute he thought they'd set up a dummy room, that she was in another room close by. But no one that looked like her had been evacuated from the rest of the floor.

Or was she dead, after all? Had they set up a room like this to draw him to her? If they had, they'd be in here now after him. Nothing made sense. His head hurt like hell, and he wanted to strike out, to do something to give vent to his rage and frustration. Then he spun around and hurried to the door. He looked out into the smokey hall, then slipped out and started for the stairwell door.

Where did they have her? Was he going to have to go through the whole hospital to find her? He reached the nurse's station that had been deserted and something stopped him in his tracks. Quickly he moved to the desk and stepped behind it. Charts. She had to have had a chart. He looked at the filing system by room numbers, but the slot for the room he was just in was empty.

Then he saw a plan manila folder lying on the desk to one side of the files. And the only thing written on the outside was a room number, the number of the room he had just been in. He picked it up and as soon as he flipped it open, he knew he'd found what he was looking for.

Her name was at the top of a release form—Lyndsey Cole. So, she was alive and well enough to leave this place. Her doctor's signature was scrawled along the bottom of the form. He'd lied. He'd sworn on television that she was comatose. So much for medical integrity, he thought and almost closed the file to go and find Dr. Levin, but stopped when he saw a notation on the side. *Released into the care of Dr. R. J. Tyler.*

R. J. Tyler. He dropped the file on the desk and looked up when he heard a commotion farther down the hall. He could make out people coming in his direction, and he moved quickly from behind the desk. Without a backward glance, he headed for the stairwell. Now all he had to do was find this R. J. Tyler and he'd find her.

Lyndsey couldn't tell what it was that intruded on her sleep sometime during the night, but she felt herself being pulled away from the comfort of peaceful rest. She tried to hold on to sleep, but she couldn't. Gradually she became aware of a noise, a soft shuffling sound, and sleep was snatched out of her grasp. She froze.

Cautiously she opened her eyes just a bit. Thankful to have the extended-wear contacts, she could see clearly. A man was by the other bed, his shadow dark and large, then he moved and pale light from the moon that drifted into the room caught the planes and angles of his face. R.J. He was picking up the pillow from the other bed.

"R.J.?" she whispered as she pushed herself up on one elbow.

He turned, the moonlight at his back making his face dark and unreadable. "I'm sorry. I was hoping I wouldn't wake you."

"I heard a sound," she said, looking up at him. "I didn't think I'd ever sleep again, but I did."

"You need it. You've been through some rough times. I'll let you get back to sleep," he said as he began to turn from her.

"R.J.?"

He stopped and looked back down at her. "Yes?"

"Aren't you going to sleep in the bed up here?"

"I thought I'd crash downstairs in front of the fire."

She sat up and relaxed back against the headboard, tugging the sheet with her. She pulled her knees to her chest and wrapped her arms around her legs. Then she rested her chin on her knees. "Did you ever catch any fish when you were here before?"

"Not one, but then I never really tried."

"What do you mean?" she asked, looking up at him.

"I went out in the boat to be alone. I never even took a fishing rod." He chuckled, an unsteady sound. "I just drifted in the boat."

"That sounds lonely," she said.

"It was. Maddy had been dead two months. I don't think I was ever lonely until she was gone." He sank down on the bed facing her and spoke through the shadows. "I came here and went to ground like a wounded animal. I was lonely as hell here, but I would have been anywhere."

She closed her eyes. "It feels as if I've been lonely all my life."

"All your life?"

"Since I can remember. Maybe that's why I married Rob. Maybe I thought the loneliness would stop." She bit her lip. "It didn't. It never did."

"There's never been a time when you weren't lonely?"

When you're with me, she wanted to say, but hedged, knowing if the words came out they would cause problems she wouldn't know how to deal with. She didn't want him to withdraw from her by saying he was her doctor and nothing more. She couldn't take that sort of rejection right now. "I guess there has been."

"Well, you aren't alone now," he said softly.

"If you go downstairs, I will be," she said simply.

"Then I'll stay," he said as he moved silently, coming to her bed and sitting on the edge. But he didn't touch her. "Maybe we can get some work done, since you're awake."

Now wasn't the time to go under and experience the guide and that feeling he gave her. She could barely deal with her feelings around R.J. when she was fully in control. "I don't think so. Can't we just talk?"

"Sure. What about?"

She spoke quickly, afraid he'd leave and go downstairs if she didn't say something to keep his attention. "Your real name."

He chuckled softly through the darkness, the sound a balm to her frayed nerves. "We're back to the name again?"

"I was thinking about it when I was taking my shower." She wouldn't mention the other thoughts that were combined with it. "And I came up with an idea."

"What is it?"

"I've been looking for exotic names, really weird names that would force you to use initials, then it hit me, maybe, just maybe, your name's simple and plain. Something like Robert James?'

"No."

"Ronald John?"

"No."

"Raymond Joseph?"

"No."

"At least tell me if I'm close."

"You aren't even in the ballpark."

"Shoot," she muttered as she sat back and rested on the wooden headboard. "I give up. Tell me what it is."

"No."

"Why not?"

"I told you, only my family and dearest friends know my real name."

That put everything in perspective. "That lets me out," she murmured and ran a hand over her face.

"Does it?" R.J. asked softly as he came closer and reached out to touch her cheek.

She was very still. "You're the doctor. I'm the patient. You're the one with all the answers," she breathed.

"You're wrong, Lyndsey, so wrong," he said, then moved even closer, his hand cupping her chin firmly, but without force.

"Is it wrong to not want to be alone?" she managed through the tightness in her throat that seemed to be spreading throughout her body, just the way the fire in his fingertips was permeating every part of her being.

"No, it's not wrong." His warm breath brushed her skin with heat.

She didn't ask if it was wrong to reach out to him, to lift her lips in an offering to his. She just did it. And for a split second she was terrified that he'd reject her, that he'd back away and leave her so lonely she was quite sure she would die from it—or from this wanting in her.

As she lifted her face, she heard R.J. inhale harshly, but the next instant, his lips were on hers. And the feeling was everything she remembered from the first kiss. Firm and gentle, hot and searching. And she opened her mouth to him, wanting him to invade her, needing more from this man than a mere kiss could give her. She wanted skin on skin, body to body.

Chapter 11

Lyndsey desperately wanted to be closer to R.J. She scrambled to her knees, circled his neck with her arms and pressed her body to his. Through the thin cotton of her sleep shirt, she felt the strength of his bare chest, and her breasts swelled, peaking and tingling. And the tingling raced to other parts of her, making her heavy with desire.

She knew in that moment that there had never been anything like this in her life. There had never been the excitement, the needing, the fear, the anticipation or the joy.

Then R.J. was easing her back into the bed, until he was lying alongside her and drawing her against him. Her body fit neatly into his, a sensation as right as any she could ever remember experiencing. She could feel the hard heat of his arousal pressing against the confines of his jeans, and his mouth was ravishing her. His lips trailed fire along the line of her jaw, to the sweep of her neck that she willingly exposed to him, and then dipped to the pulse that beat frantically in the hollow of her throat.

His hands were touching her, through the thin cotton of her shirt, and every spot he felt came to life. He swept the curve of her hips with his hand, flicking over the bare skin of her legs, skimming past the elastic of her panty leg, then up under the cotton of her sleep shirt. When skin touched skin, Lyndsey gasped from the pleasure the contact gave her.

R.J. smothered her cry with his mouth, his tongue tracing the smoothness of her teeth, while his hand spanned the breadth of her stomach, then moved upward. She held her breath, waiting, wanting, then R.J.'s hand found the full swelling of her breasts. His fingers traced the circle of her nipple as it peaked and hardened. Lost in pleasure, she threw her head back, her eyes closed, and she felt as if she was the center of the universe and filled with joy she had only dreamed about up until now.

Then R.J. was pushing aside the flimsy cotton barrier, and his mouth covered the spot his hand had just left. When she felt the soft tugging on her nipple, the heat and moisture, a sob broke from her lips, and she wondered if anyone had ever died from sheer pleasure. And at the moment, she knew if she did, she wouldn't regret one moment of this time with R.J.

Her shirt was higher, almost up to her neck, and R.J. moved back to look at her. A faintly cool breeze brushed her exposed breasts, making the ache in them more acute, almost painful. And she arched upward, needing his hands on her, needing that heat and contact the way a drowning man needs a life preserver.

"You're beautiful," R.J. whispered through the shadows as his touch came back to her, lovingly gentle, kneading and massaging, building feelings in her that threatened to make her fragment. Then his hands moved from her breasts, and she almost cried out with disappointment, until she felt his touch on her. She closed her eyes, focusing entirely on the points where they were joined, letting that become the full focus of her being.

She'd never experienced anything like this. She'd heard about it, the all-consuming need of one person for another, yet it had never been a reality in her life. With Rob there had been little pleasure, and mostly pain. He'd never been gentle and caring, not even at first. Sex had been something to do for him, to give him satisfaction, but never for her to enjoy and find release.

And she'd thought it was her fault, that she wasn't sexy enough, that she wasn't capable of wild abandonment. Their encounters had been mere minutes, but had felt like an unending eternity for Lyndsey. She could remember praying to have it over with so Rob would roll away from her and leave her alone.

Now she prayed for it never to end, for these feelings to go on and on, that she'd feel R.J.'s body against hers forever, that she'd know him completely and fully. Then his hand went lower, his fingertips slipping under the elastic of her panties, and her breath caught in her throat. His touch set her on fire, scrambling all of her thoughts, except one that cut through like a shard of jagged glass.

A memory of those last months with Rob. Rob trying to take her, forcing her, hissing that she was his, and he'd do what he wanted to do. And he hadn't been able to do anything. But the memory was in the bed with her now, piercing her to the heart, and threatening to kill every good feeling growing in her.

She wanted to arch to R.J., to raise her hips, to press herself against him and feel him with her. But as his hand went lower, sliding under her panties, she froze. She felt fear, as great as any fear she'd experienced during this nightmare. And she hated Rob for robbing her of the ability to just let herself go.

He'd victimized her in more ways than she'd ever dreamed possible.

With a sob, she rolled away from R.J., pressing her face into the pillows and pulling her knees to her stomach. "No," she gasped. "I can't."

R.J. didn't speak and didn't touch her, but she felt his heat at her back, and she almost wished she could die. There was such promise in his touch, but not for her. She tugged her top down to cover herself. Damn Rob, damn him, she wanted to scream, and struck the pillow with her tight fist.

"Lyndsey, I'm sorry. I didn't mean—"

She waved aside his words weakly with her hand, and she tried to find words to tell him what had happened, words that made sense. "I can't let you . . ." She pressed her hand to her mouth. "I'm sorry . . ."

The darkness was all around, then R.J. spoke softly, whispering words that brought tears to her eyes. "Is it all right if I just hold you?"

Oh, God, she wanted that more than life itself, to be held and not to be alone, to feel him with her.

His hand touched her shoulder, its heat beckoning to her. "That's all," he whispered close to her ear. "I just want to hold you close so you won't be alone."

As seductive as his touch had been just moments ago, his words were even more compelling. And she needed what he was offering, she needed it desperately. She went to him, rolling back to face him, and with an ease that made her heart ache, she found herself in his arms, held tightly against the length of his body.

Then tears came. Tears of anger, tears of frustration and tears for what she would never know. Even though she loved him, she couldn't ever be with him.

Love? Yes, she admitted it, she recognized it, but she was filled with sorrow that she wasn't capable of ever having a loving relationship. "It takes two to love," R.J. had said, and he'd been right. He wanted her, but he couldn't love her. He probably wouldn't ever love again, and she probably wouldn't ever love anyone but him for the rest of her life.

She pressed her face into his bare chest, which was damp with her tears. She gulped air, then snuggled closer to R.J., allowing herself to hold onto him, thankful that she wouldn't be alone tonight.

R.J. felt Lyndsey shudder against him, then with a sigh, she rested her arm on his waist and pressed her face to his chest. Gradually he could feel her begin to relax, then ever so slowly slip into a light sleep. He stayed very still, holding her, but the burning passion that had been there moments ago shocked him in the way it had shifted and changed. Now all he wanted to do was heal her. To make whatever was wrong right. And to free her of the hold her ex-husband's abuse still had on her.

He shifted, his body still uncomfortable with evidence of needs that hadn't been met, and he stroked Lyndsey's silky hair. For a long time, he stared at the shadows of the ceiling over the bed, thankful he'd been stopped before he'd allowed himself to make love with her. She'd kept him from compromising everything he held dear professionally.

This wouldn't happen again. As soon as he could, he'd make sure there wouldn't be a problem that way. But overriding all of that was the wonder he felt that in a place where he had died a thousand deaths, he felt as if he had been given a way to live again.

R.J. slept fitfully that night, a fitfulness born of worry, frustration and the fact that every time he shifted, he felt Lyndsey beside him. She snuggled into his side, as trusting as a child, but with all the potent sexuality of a woman. And he couldn't ignore it.

When dawn crept into the room, he carefully disentangled himself from Lyndsey's arms, making sure he didn't waken her, then he slipped out of bed. The cold air of morning brushed his skin, but he didn't notice. He paused to look down at Lyndsey in sleep, that vulnerability he'd seen before even more potent for him now.

He turned away from the sight and headed downstairs, stopping in the living room to lay a new fire and get it started before going into the kitchen to use the phone. He knew Russ well enough to know he wouldn't still be at home at seven in the morning, so he called police headquarters and asked for Russ's extension. It rang just once before he heard Russ answer. "Homicide, Detective MacClain."

"Russ, it's me."

"What's wrong, R.J.?" Russ said quickly.

"Nothing to do with the case," R.J. said. "I just called to ask you how you got so damned smart?"

"What are you talking about?"

"You were right. I can't stay on this case as Lyndsey's doctor any longer."

"So, that's the way it is?"

"It sure is." R.J. closed his eyes to the soft light of morning filtering into the kitchen. How could he say these things to Russ? Russ was Maddy's brother. How could he tell her brother that another woman was working her way into his life and into his heart? How could he tell him that he felt guilty and sad and excited and scared all at the same time? Yet he knew that if anyone could understand, it was Russ.

"What happened?" Russ asked.

He hedged. "A lot. But the main thing is, I'm on the verge of compromising everything and everyone."

"It sounds to me as if you're just coming back to the land of the living," Russ murmured.

"For better or worse."

"I don't know if I'm mad at you or happy for you. The best thing that can happen to you is to get out and live again. But the worst thing for me is having you leave this case right now."

"I'm walking out on the case, not Lyndsey," he said, getting the words out while he still could. "I'm in this until the end, but I'm staying on the basis of being your friend and helping you out of a jam. No more doctor and patient. No more professional consultation."

"Is this mutual?" Russ asked.

"She's been through hell and she's scared to death." He sucked in air. "And she's not ready for any kind of relationship just yet. She needs time, and I've got plenty of it. I'll tell you all about it when this is over, but I can't, not yet. I just wanted to get off this case, to be formally removed."

"You've got it. I'll put it in the computer. You're off the payroll even as we speak. Good enough?"

"Good enough," he said, feeling as if a weight the size of the world had been lifted off his shoulders. But it was replaced with something else. He had no idea where he was going or what would happen to him when he got there. But the shocking thing was, he wanted to take that chance.

"R.J.?"

"Yeah?"

"I need to tell you something. It might not mean a thing, but it could."

"What?"

"There was a fire at the hospital last night, on the floor below the one Lyndsey was staying on. It started in a closet where they kept supplies. We can't be sure, but it looks as if it was deliberately set."

"Why?"

"I didn't know at first, then we went back to the dummy room. The door was open. The cop on duty swears it was closed tight when he evacuated."

"Someone was checking to make sure no one was left behind." That sounded logical to R.J.

"Maybe, or maybe our guy set the fire to get us out of the way so he could find out if Lyndsey was in there." That sounded just as logical to R.J. "If that's the case," Russ continued, "he knows she's out and around."

"What now?"

"Nothing. Just do what you can . . . for a friend, and do it as quickly as you can. I need answers, and I need them badly."

"I'll try."

"Thanks. Be careful," Russ said, then hung up.

R.J. put the phone back, then pressed both hands flat on the cold tile of the counter and took a deep breath. He was alive. He turned and walked back toward the stairs through the silent house. For a moment he stopped at the bottom of the stairs and listened.

There were no sounds. Lyndsey was still asleep. He thought of putting on his shirt and shoes and going for a walk to try to clear his thoughts in the morning air, then he knew he couldn't. He remembered last night, how worried Lyndsey had been about being left alone and the promise he'd given her not to leave without telling her. He meant to keep that promise. As he slowly climbed the stairs, he made another promise to himself that he intended to keep.

Lyndsey Cole was going to live happily ever after. Even if it wasn't with him, she'd live a life in which she was loved and cherished. And he'd do whatever it took to make good on that promise.

The lone man found Dr. R. J. Tyler's phone number and office address in the yellow pages of the phone book under Psychiatrists. A head doctor? Someone to help her deal with what had happened? Someone to get answers out of her? If that was the case, he didn't have much time.

He picked up the phone in a side office near the maintenance area of the hospital and dialed the number for Dr. Tyler. After three rings, a woman answered. "Good morning. Dr. Tyler's office."

"Hello. This is Dr. Larson calling for Dr. Tyler." He'd seen the name on the registry, another psychiatrist on staff at the hospital.

"I'm sorry, but Dr. Tyler isn't available. Can I take a message and have him get back to you?"

"No, that's all right. I'll call him back in a few hours."

"That wouldn't do any good, I'm afraid. Doctor's out of the office for a while."

"I don't understand. He asked me to call for a consultation for my patient, and I'm certain he didn't say anything about being gone for any length of time."

"It was sort of sudden."

"There's nothing wrong, is there?"

"No, not at all. Actually he's gone fishing. You know what he's been through since his wife died. Well, he's finally taking time to enjoy himself. He left a message with the service last night that he'd be gone for a few days."

He felt his stomach clench so tightly that he could taste sickness in his throat. Fishing? What was going on? He worked at making himself sound pleased for the man. "I know exactly what you mean. He deserves the time off. I hope he got reservations on such short notice?"

"He wouldn't need them. He went to a lodge on the island."

"The island?" he asked, holding his breath.

"Lyon Island in the Sound. A friend of his has a lodge there."

"He must be a good friend."

"He is. Dr. Tyler's known Bob Hanlahan for years."

"Well, thanks for your help. I'll call back in a few days to see if he's returned." Before she could say anything else, he hung up and put the receiver back in place. He had all the information he needed. He stared at the phone and repeated softly to himself, "Lyon Island. So, she was on Lyon Island with the good doctor?

Lyndsey drifted out of sleep slowly and gently, and she assumed R.J. was nearby. But when she shifted, she knew he wasn't beside her; he wasn't holding her or whispering soft comfort to her the way he had when she'd roused during the night.

There was no heat against her, no sound of his deep, regular breathing. Yet she could sense his presence close by, much the way she had felt the presence of the guide. She shifted onto her back, felt brightness against her closed lids, then slowly opened her eyes.

That moment was almost a repeat of the time at the hospital when she'd put on her glasses. R.J. had been at the foot of her bed, and she'd seen him clearly for the first time. Now, with her contacts in, she could see R.J. at the foot of the bed watching her. The sun was coming in through the dormers behind him, the brightness blurring his silhouette and making his image almost ethereal.

Lyndsey felt a catch in her heart as she looked up at him and took in the chambray shirt unbuttoned and loose from the jeans, its sleeves rolled up to show strong forearms. His eyes were in shadow and unreadable.

Her response to just the sight of the man was every bit as strong as her response to his touch last night. Last night. She felt a flood of embarrassment wash over her as she remembered what had happened, and she looked away. As she reached for the sheet to pull it higher, she felt heat in her face. How could she have frozen like that?

"I was wondering if you'd ever wake up," R.J. said as he came around and sat opposite her on the other bed. She glanced toward him, seeing the sheets and blankets still intact on that bed. Despite how she'd reacted to him, he'd stayed with her all night.

She touched her tongue to her lips. "What time is it?" she asked.

"It's just after noon."

"Oh, goodness," she said, pushing herself up until she was sitting, and she made very sure she tugged the sheet up with her. She held the fabric to her chest with one hand and tried to smooth her hair with the other. "I'm sorry. I didn't mean to sleep so late."

"You needed it," he said.

Yes, she did, she needed the rest. She brushed at her eyes, then made herself look at R.J., and she knew what she really needed to do. "I need to explain about last night," she said, marveling that her voice was fairly steady.

"No, you don't. I was out of line. I apologize for that."

She stared at him. "You? No, you weren't. I asked you to stay. I practically threw myself at you, then I...I couldn't..." She bit her lip hard. "You have to understand, I wanted to. I mean, it wasn't you. It was me. I was scared. I never..." She twisted the sheet she had clutched in her hands, knowing she had to make R.J. understand. "Rob, he was crazy. He wasn't gentle at all. He was..."

R.J. moved to come and sit by her on the bed, touching her on her hands to make them still on the sheets. "You don't have to explain."

She looked at him, seeing pity in his eyes. She didn't want that from him, just understanding. "I do," she whispered and closed her eyes tightly, then tangled her fingers with R.J.'s. She held on to him for dear life while she told him things that she hadn't told another human being, not even Estelle.

She told him about Rob, about what he did, what he made her do, words spilling out one over the other in a rush. The ugliness threatened to choke her, but she forced the words to be said, words that she knew had to be said if R.J. was ever going to understand what happened.

When she didn't have anything else inside her to say, she gulped to a stop and stared at her hands tangled with R.J.'s. When he didn't say anything for what seemed forever, she tried to pull away from him, but he wouldn't let her. Then, with a low expletive that shook her, he drew her to him and silently held her in the circle of his arms, rocking her back and forth as if she were a small child who'd fallen down and skinned her knee. But she wasn't a child. And it wasn't her knee that was damaged, it was her soul.

She felt R.J. stroke her hair, then he spoke softly, his words vibrating against her cheek pressed to his chest. "God help me, the man's sick. He's an animal, and if I could, I'd have him shot. What he did to you..." He took a shuddering breath, then said, "Don't let him keep victimizing you. Let go of him, and put him in the past. That's where he belongs. He's gone. He's nothing to you now. You have to let go. You have to forget he exists."

She shook her head, rubbing her forehead against his chest where the cotton of his shirt parted. "You don't understand. I can't."

He moved back, cupping her chin with one hand and gently making her look up at him. His dark eyes were filled with such intensity that it shocked her. "It was him, Lyndsey, not you. You didn't do a thing to deserve what he put you through. You have to know that, believe that and forget about him." His hand tightened. "You have to."

"You don't understand," she said, tears burning her eyes. "He won't let me."

"What?"

"He won't let me. He's going to kill me."

R.J. froze, his hand on her not moving. "Those are threats made by a crazy person. He won't try to kill you."

She moved away from the contact with R.J., going back until she felt the coldness of the headboard behind her. "The last time I saw him, he told me he'd get me, he'd find me. He found me in the shelter I had to go to when I left him. You know they keep those places hidden. They don't give out addresses or phone numbers, not even to family members. But he found me there. He said he'd make me sorry I didn't go back to him."

R.J. shook his head. "Words, just words, another way of abusing you and intimidating you."

"No, he meant it. I know he did."

"Lyndsey, listen to me." He reached out to her again, but before he could touch her, she was saying words she never thought she would say.

"It was him, R.J., it was Rob who tried to kill me."

His hand stilled in midair. "What are you talking about?"

"I know it was Rob who attacked me at the garage. You all thought it was the killer, but I know it was Rob."

R.J. sat very still, his hand falling down to rest on his thigh. "You're telling me that you knew all along that your ex-husband tried to kill you and you told no one? You went through hypnosis, through all of that, and you knew all the time?" He stood, towering over her. "All this time—"

"No," she said quickly. "I really didn't remember. I can't remember. When I think back to when I turned, it's all blank. But in my gut I know it was Rob."

"How do you know?"

"I don't know how." She shook her head. "I just do."

"Why didn't you tell Russ all of this?"

She looked away from R.J. and narrowed her eyes against the brightness of the light pouring in the dormer windows. "I was afraid if the one who attacked me was the killer and I told the police about Rob, they'd get in touch with Rob, and he'd find out where I was."

"They'd have kept your whereabouts secret."

"They'd say they would, but the police seldom do what they say they'll do. I know that. If it wasn't for Estelle at the woman's shelter, I'd still be with Rob. I just didn't know for sure, and I couldn't take that chance."

"All this time, you thought it was Rob?"

She looked back up at R.J. "Yes. That's why I called him to find out if he was in Dallas. He wasn't. They said he was gone, taking time off. He never took time off. He's here in Seattle, and he's coming after me."

R.J. dropped down on the bed again, not more than two feet from Lyndsey. "You're saying you have something in you that's telling you the attacker is Rob, that it's just a coincidence that the B & B Strangler has the same MO, that he goes after women who look like you?"

"I know that sounds crazy, but, yes. I don't know what it is, but I'm sure it was Rob who tried to kill me. It has to be him."

He looked right at her. "Do you want to find out for sure?" he asked.

"That's why I've been doing all of this to try to remember. I *need* to know for sure. If it's Rob, I have to get out of here and disappear. If it's the killer after me, I have to find out so I can help Russ stop him."

"Then let's do it."

"How?"

"First, you have to trust Russ. Can you do that?"

She didn't know. Russ seemed like a nice enough man when he wasn't tied up in knots about this case. But it was her life. Or what life she hoped she could have. "I don't know."

"Do you trust me?"

That answer came more easily than anything had for a very long time. "Yes."

"Then I'm telling you that you can trust Russ MacClain with your life. I'd trust him with mine."

"But what could he do?"

"He can find out where Rob is and never even let Rob know he's being investigated. Just give me Rob's full name and his address, and I'll call Russ and explain everything to him."

She felt real relief now she'd told R.J. everything, and she quickly told him where Rob lived and where he worked. When he stood to go and call Russ, Lyndsey looked up at him. "You'll explain to Russ why I didn't tell him the truth, won't you, and make sure he doesn't let Rob know where I am . . . if he's in Dallas?"

"Sure." With an ease that should have come only after years of being together, R.J. bent over Lyndsey, cupped her chin in his hand and touched his lips to her forehead. "I'll take care of everything," he whispered, then straightened and headed downstairs.

The lone man saw the island across the Sound, the chunk of land rising with green richness out of the cool blueness of the water. And he felt excitement rise up in him. He was close, so close. Once she was dead, he could move on. He'd be free for a while. He saw the ferry right ahead and drove his car up and onto the deck. He watched other cars come on board, parking behind him and to his right. Then as the ferry motor started, he sat back in his seat.

He stared straight ahead at the island and took a stick of gum out of his pocket. He unwrapped the gum, popped it into his mouth, then slowly rolled the foil into a tight ball between his thumb and forefinger. He put down the window, flipped the foil out, and watched it arch through the air toward the water.

As the island came closer and closer, he felt a rush of excitement, the same feeling he got when he felt in total control of himself and everything around him. And he was in control again, at least he would be when he headed back to the mainland on this ferry. Lyndsey Cole would be dead.

Chapter 12

As R.J. stood in the kitchen with the phone pressed to his ear listening to Russ give vent to his anger on the other end of the line, he stared out the windows. He was watching Shields and Magee across the lawn behind the house. Except for the bulge of their guns under their jackets, they could have been any two men enjoying the clear autumn day.

"I had a gut feeling she was lying," Russ was muttering over the phone as his burst of anger began to die out.

"That's just it, Russ," he said when he had a chance to get a word in edgewise. "She wasn't lying. She just didn't tell you about the husband. And you can understand why. You came in there like a madman." He heard the upstairs shower start. "Russ, she's terrified of her ex. He's an animal. If you looked up the word abuser in the dictionary, his picture would be there. What matters is that I promised her you could check on this guy without him ever knowing you're checking. Was I right?"

There was a long silence, then a grudging, "Yeah, you're right."

"Good." The two men outside had stopped to talk for a few minutes, then turned and headed for the house. "You find out where Rob Peters is, and I'll do what I can on this end to find out what Lyndsey really knows."

"What do you think about this, R.J.? Are we looking for the B & B Strangler in her case, or an angry ex-husband?"

"I don't know. Whoever's after Lyndsey *is* trying to kill her. I don't think it matter if it's a stranger or her ex-husband." He heard footsteps on the front porch. "I'll be waiting to hear from you."

He hung up, went back through the house to the front door and pulled it open. Larry Shields, a friend of Russ's in Homicide, was coming up to the door. In a dark jacket and wool watch hat, the short, blocky man had the face of a cop—sober and tense. Dan Magee was younger and larger, a barrel-chested man who had been on the force for just over five years. The quilted plaid jacket he was wearing emphasized his large build, and the bright orange hunter's hat stood out like a beacon against the cool green of the surrounding land.

"Is everything okay in there?" Shields asked.

"Fine. How about outside?"

"So far, so good. We walked the property, and the two weak points are the drive and the back entrance down to the beach. We'll split up and keep them both covered." He came closer and handed R.J. a small two-way radio. "Detective MacClain said to give you this. Keep this with you all the time, and use it to get in touch if you need us."

"Thanks," R.J. said.

"Let us know if you leave the house."

"Sure."

"We'll be around outside."

R.J. nodded, then stepped back and closed the door. Footsteps on the stairs behind him let him know that Lyndsey was coming down. He turned, and the sight of her dressed in jeans, a loose blue sweater over a blouse and tennis shoes, made his chest tighten. How could a man do what Rob Peters had done to her? She was made to be cherished and protected and loved. Yes, loved, he thought as she stopped on the bottom step.

"Who was at the door?" she asked.

"Our two friends." He held up the tiny radio. "We're to keep in touch."

"Did you talk to Russ?"

"Yes. He's going to check and get back as soon as he knows anything."

"Was he angry?"

"That pretty much sums it up. I think you should know that he thought you were lying or hiding something from the start."

Her face was stained with bright color. "I'm so sorry. I didn't know who I could trust, and I was scared."

"I know. It's been hell for you, but don't worry, I made him understand that your theory that the killer is Rob was only a hunch, that you really didn't have a memory of the attacker's face."

Her fine eyebrows drew together in a frown. "It's blank. There's nothing when I try to visualize it." She hesitated, then said, "I've been thinking it over, and I think I should let you try using drugs on me."

That was the last thing he expected. "Why?"

"You've tried hypnosis and talking, and it's gotten us nowhere. Russ is no closer to catching whoever did this than he was when they found me. I'm willing to try anything."

"Not drugs."

"Why not? You're the one who suggested them before."

He backed away from it. "I know, but it's not feasible right now. It would have to be done in a hospital environment, and that's impossible."

She sank slowly down onto the step and buried her face in her hands. "Then what are we going to do?" She dropped her hands and looked up at him with wide blue eyes. "I need to know if Rob's the one so I can get away from here if he is."

"You'll run again?" R.J. asked as he dropped to his haunches in front of her.

"I have to."

"Russ can take care of Rob."

"No, he can't." She looked him in the eye, and he saw the depth of the pain the man had inflicted on her. "He probably couldn't prove it, and *if* he could, Rob could be out of jail in a matter of months. I can't take that sort of chance."

"Where will you go?" he asked, shocked at the pain that was settling in his chest at the thought of her running all her life.

"I don't know. Someplace far away. Someplace where Rob can never find me."

"You're getting ahead of things. Let's take this one step at a time. Let Russ do his job, and you can work on remembering. Maybe this whole thing will be over sooner than any of us think."

"I hope so," she murmured, getting to her feet and stepping past him to go into the living room. She walked silently to the spyglass and looked through the eyepiece out the window.

R.J. stared at her, at the slender lines and angles of her body, at the way her hair curled slightly on the exposed nape of her neck, and at the delicate shape of her fingers on the polished brass. How had this happened to him? How had he let this woman work her way into his heart? That was something he was never going to allow again, something he would have sworn would never happen again, but after last night, after that first touch, he knew how dangerously close he was to really caring.

"There are men out there," she said, straightening and looking at him.

"Does one have on a brilliant orange hunter's hat?"

She looked through the spyglass again. "Yes, and a plaid coat. He's a big man. The other one's shorter with dark clothes."

"The one with the hat is Dan Magee. The other one is Larry Shields, our bodyguards." He strode past her to the kitchen door. "I hope you can cook, because I'm terrible at it," he said over his shoulder.

"I can open a can with the best of them," he heard her murmur as she came up behind him.

Without looking back at her, he pushed open the kitchen door and found himself smiling. "Good, Bob's got a state-of-the-art can opener somewhere in this kitchen."

Lyndsey ate the last piece of toast and looked down at her plate. Everything was gone, the eggs, the toast, and the fruit. She hadn't guessed she was hungry until that first bite, then she had been ravenous. It was the first good food she'd had in a long time. She pushed back her empty plate, then looked up at R.J. He was sipping coffee, the mug cradled in both hands, and watching her over the rim.

"Had enough?" he asked.

"More than enough." She sat back with a sigh and patted her stomach. "I don't remember when I ever ate that much for breakfast."

He stood and reached for the plates, stacking them along with the silverware. "You're not a breakfast person?"

"I'm not a morning person," she admitted.

He took the dishes to the sink, put them in with a clatter, then turned and smiled at her. "This isn't morning anymore."

"It sure isn't," she said, looking away from his smile, which made her feel slightly light-headed. She pushed her chair back from the table and stood. "We're wasting time. Let's get on with this."

He came toward her. "You need to relax a bit. It could help you remember. Why don't we got for a walk on the beach?"

The idea appealed to her, just to walk on the beach in the fresh air with R.J. and forget about all of this. But she couldn't. "No, I want you to hypnotize me. Get me to go past the blank in my memory."

He shook his head. "I can't."

"What do you mean, you can't."

"I can't."

"You did. You have to do it again. I promise I'll keep going this time. I won't let anything stop me from seeing the attacker's face."

"Lyndsey, I have to tell you something."

She didn't understand what was going on. "What?"

"I'm not on this case any longer."

None of this made sense. "You're what?"

"I called Russ this morning and dropped off the case. He took me off the payroll."

Her mind was spinning. "What do you mean, you dropped off the case? You're here. You're supposed to be helping me."

"Since I'm not officially your doctor anymore, I can't do hypnosis on you."

She didn't understand anything, except she felt as if she'd been totally deserted. She'd let herself trust him, depend on him, and now he was saying he was walking away. "You can't just stop like that. What am I going to do?"

"We'll talk, and maybe you can work past the block that way," was all he said before he turned and went into the living room.

She ran after him and caught up with him in front of the fireplace. She reached out, grabbing him by the arm and stopping him. When he turned, she drew her hand back. She felt suddenly cold, and the fire in the hearth didn't touch her with its heat. "I don't understand any of this, why you won't be on the case anymore, or what's wrong, but I'm begging you to hypnotize me. Please."

He looked down at her, his hazel eyes narrowed, his dark brows drawn together in a frown. "I don't think so."

"Then why are you here at all?" she demanded, feeling as if she was coming apart at the seams. She need him here, with her, to see her through this to the end. "Why aren't you on a ferry heading back to the mainland?"

"For personal reasons. As a favor to Russ, an old friend, to help him."

As he said the words, she knew they weren't what she wanted to hear. She wanted to hear that he cared about her, that he had stayed for her, that he'd taken himself off the case because he wanted to make love with her and couldn't while he was still on it. But those were her fantasies, not reality. And her regret at not being able to make love last night only deepened. She felt reality settle around her like a shroud. "Then hypnotize me as a favor to me. We can pretend we're friends . . . for a little while, can't we?"

He touched her gently on the cheek with just the tip of his forefinger, touching her skin in a feather-light contact. "Is that what you really want, for us to be friends?"

"Yes," she breathed, feeling as if she had just defined all she could ever have from R.J.

He drew back and pushed his hands into the pockets of his jeans. "Let's get things set up."

Lyndsey chose the bed so she could recline, supported with pillows at her back and head, just as she did in the chair. R.J. found a chair from downstairs, brought it up and put it by the bed at the same angle the chair at the hospital had been positioned.

R.J. pulled the curtains over the windows while Lyndsey settled on the bed, then came back to sit in the chair. "Whenever you're ready," he said.

She closed her eyes, rested her hands on her thighs, then felt R.J. touch her shoulder. "I'm ready," she whispered.

"Just relax. Breathe in and out." His hand pressure matched her breathing pattern. "Let yourself go to the safe place."

This time it happened so fast, from the first words for her to relax until she was in the "safe place" and the guide was by her, just out of her line of sight.

"When you're ready to go further, just let me know," R.J.'s voice said.

Lyndsey felt the presence of the guide, an aura of heat and security emanating from him. She stood on the sand, looking out over the ocean, then slowly she turned toward the guide. Afraid when she looked he'd vanish, she almost stopped herself, then she kept going, and she saw him.

R.J. Standing, looking at her. R.J. in soft light, talking to her, his words echoing inside her, yet his lips weren't moving. "You knew it was me all along, didn't you?" he asked her deep in her being.

"Yes," she whispered. "I knew."

He smiled, but even though he didn't touch her, she could feel him in her soul. "Are you ready to go?"

"If you're going to be with me."

"Always," he said, the voice echoing in her. "Always."

She was drifting, back, back, to that Friday. Drifting as if in a haze that enveloped her and protected her. And R.J. was with her every step of the way.

"Where are you?" the other voice of R.J. asked, the voice that surrounded her.

"Friday. At work."

"Skip ahead as far as you can."

She did. Going to the afternoon. Leaving work, going to the bank, then coming out and being bumped and having her glasses knocked off. She bent over, picked up her glasses, then put them on. Embarrassed, she tried not to look, but she heard him. "Sorry," he muttered, and she took a quick slanting look to her right before she walked off. A large man with pale hair, rough skin, and eyes hidden behind dark glasses.

Turning away, she was hurrying to her car, getting inside.

"Where are you now?"

"In the car."

"Where are you going?"

"To the apartment."

"What are you seeing and thinking?"

"I see the Sound off in the distance, bright sun. And I'm thinking that I hate my glasses, that I wish I hadn't torn my contact. And I'm thinking that it seems like Rob was in another lifetime. I see the apartment building."

"Keep going."

Right in front, turning toward the parking entrance. "I'm going to park."

She was driving into the parking area, the sunlight changing to soft, diffused light. The structure almost empty. No one around. Parking the car. Stopping the engine. Putting keys in my pocket. Looking in the mirror.

"Tell me what's going on," the outside voice was saying.

"I'm looking in the mirror, happy not to be with Rob, having a new life. I'm touching the door handle."

The inner voice was there. "I'm with you. I'm with you all the way," it said softly in her soul.

She pulled the handle, pushed open the door, got out.

"Are you out of the car?" the outer voice asked.

"Yes, standing by it, reaching back inside for my purse." Fear tugged at her, that knowledge that something was coming, but being unable to stop it. Then the inner voice was louder. "You're safe. I'm with you. Forever."

"Lyndsey, keep talking to me," the outer voice persisted.

"I . . . I know someone's there," she said.

"How do you know, Lyndsey?" the outer voice said.

"I know." And she did. It was Rob. She knew it. Yet she hadn't turned. The hand was on her, clamped on her upper arm, jerking her back out of the car, covering her mouth and nose with his hand. Hitting and kicking at him, feeling his hold slip, then the crushing band of his arm around her middle.

Taking a jerky breath before his hand was smothering her. Then going forward, striking the car, being grabbed and spinning around.

"Talk to me, Lyndsey, talk to me."

"I'm here," the inner voice kept saying, "I won't leave you."

She turned, her need to see who was hurting her overriding her fear. But she didn't see anything. Red, raw pain exploded through her head. A pain such as she'd never known before. And she cried out, then the guide had her, and she felt him holding her, and she seemed to be disappearing into him.

The garage was gone, the chill and dimness finished, and she was in a place she never wanted to leave, a place she had been looking for all her life. And she held to it as the soft whispers of assurance floated through her and around her and the pain was gone.

Then the outer voice was there. "Lyndsey, I'm bringing you out of it."

But she was thinking, "No, please, no," and tried to ignore the words. But she found that she couldn't. No matter how much she wanted to hold on to the illusions of the moment, she had to let go. She had to release the guide and slip back to reality.

But as she heard R.J. count backward, she found that illusion and reality blended together in the most potent way. As she came closer to reality, as she heard R.J. say "two," then "one," she found that he was holding her. It wasn't just in the dream, or just as her guide. And she was holding him so tightly her arms hurt.

They were together on the bed with her attached to R.J., encompassed in heat and security that was being replaced by a need that had only begun to materialize the night before. She kept her eyes closed, pressing her forehead into his chest.

"Are you all right?" he whispered against her hair.

"There was pain everywhere," she said, her voice muffled against his chest. "But something I know. Something was there...but I...I can't catch it and hold it."

"When did you realize it?" he asked, his voice a deep rumble against her as he spoke.

"When I was being jerked backward. I took a breath, and it was there. And I knew...I knew if I turned I'd see Rob, but when I did, I hurt all over, in my head and shoulders. And it was blank, except for the pain." She shook her head, rubbing her forehead against his chest. "God, it's blank, R.J., just blank."

He held her tightly, his one hand stroking her head in the most comforting way. "You'll get past it. You just have to give yourself time."

She pushed back, looking up at R.J. "We don't have time, you know that. Life's short, but this makes it seem as if it could all be over in seconds, in the next beat of your heart."

"You're right," he said in a low voice. "That's exactly what life is all about. That's why I dropped out of the official case. That's why I'm still here," he said, then in the next heartbeat, was lowering his head to hers.

Lyndsey lifted her lips to the kiss, needing it, wanting it, and when she parted her lips as his heat touched her, she felt him groan. Then he was kissing her with an aching tenderness that almost brought tears to her eyes. He was the guide, with all the gentleness and beauty, and he was a real man with passion and hunger that she felt echoed in her.

She was kissing him back, opening her mouth, inviting his invasion, feeling a desperation to know this man in the fullest sense of the word. It scared her and excited her, and she wound her arms around his neck, pulling him to her so tightly she could barely breathe.

She wanted him, and she wanted him now, and she didn't want to freeze again, pull back and stop this. With suffocating urgency, she kissed him hard, only to find him pulling away. And she felt choked with embarrassment as R.J. moved back enough to catch her face between his hands. His thumbs moved slowly on her cheeks, then she opened her eyes and looked at him.

"I'm sorry," she whispered unsteadily.

"No," he breathed, "don't be. We've got time." He touched his lips to her, the contact feathery soft and totally unsatisfactory to Lyndsey, but before she could move closer to have more, he drew back. "I stepped down professionally from the case because I knew that sometime, someplace, I'd want nothing more than to make love to you."

She felt tears prick the back of her eyes. "After what happened last time?"

His thumbs moved in slow, hypnotic circles on her cheeks, and when he spoke, the heat of his breath brushed her face. "I said 'make love,' Lyndsey, not just have sex, not get my own satisfaction. I want to show you the difference."

Every part of her crystallized into a need for this man. But she also felt fear. "I'm afraid I'll disappoint you," she admitted, feeling the heat of embarrassment in her face.

"You? Never," he said in low voice. "There isn't a chance of that happening."

A shiver rippled through her when she thought of how little she'd had to give in the past. "But, I—"

His voice was low and hoarse. "Do you want me?"

The question was so foolish to her that she could have laughed. But the expression in his eyes made her tremble instead. "Yes," she breathed, "I want you."

"Thank you," he said, and she knew she should be the one thanking him. Then his hands were moving to her shoulders, trailing to the buttons on her blouse. Without looking away from her face, R.J. slowly unbuttoned each fastener, and when his fingers brushed her bare skin under the cotton, she sucked in air.

That brought a smile to his lips, an expression that faltered when she began to echo his movements. With fingers that almost wouldn't cooperate, she undid the buttons on his shirt. Her blouse parted, falling open, and her hands on R.J.'s shirt stilled. She felt the cool air of the room brush her bare skin, then R.J. was slipping her blouse off her shoulders.

She closed her eyes, momentarily embarrassed to be exposed to this man, then she felt his hands on the fastener of her bra and she felt her breath catch in her chest. In a moment, the flimsy lace of the bra was gone, slipping off in a tangle with her blouse. And she sat very still, then opened her eyes to R.J.

"Lord, you're beautiful," he breathed. Then his hands were cupping the weight of her breasts. "I never knew anything could be this soft and silky."

"I never knew anything could feel like this," she said, biting her lip and closing her eyes as his fingers found her nipples and teased them into peaks.

"This is just the beginning." His voice had dropped to a rough, unsteady whisper. "Just the beginning."

She reached for his shirt, fumbling with the remaining buttons, then tugging the cotton off so she could spread her hands on his chest and feel his heat under her fingers. And as she pressed her hands to his chest, she felt him shudder.

With a low groan, he pushed back, getting off the bed to strip off his jeans and expose the hard desire that echoed in her. She had no more than a heartbeat to take in the sight of him naked before he was back with her and they were tumbling into the covers.

R.J. wanted nothing more than to take her right then. To fill her and know her and feel that release that he had wanted since he'd first touched her and felt that shock of awareness course through him. But he knew he couldn't. He knew he had to take it slow and easy, that he had to give and give and give, until she wanted him as badly as he wanted her.

The damage Rob had done was monumental, but R.J. would take as much time as was needed to make Lyndsey know how much she moved him, how sexy she was, and how desirable she was. If she could only understand that she could drive him mad with just a look. But to touch her, to lie with her, was overwhelming.

He rolled onto his side, supporting himself on his elbow, and looked down at her in the soft light of early evening. Her beauty tugged at him, filling his body, and he touched her cheek, unnerved to see the way his hand was shaking. "We'll take it slow and easy, all right?"

She nodded, her tongue darting out to touch her lips. Then she was hesitantly touching his cheek, her fingers were on his lips, and she traced the line of his mouth. "Kiss me," she whispered, "please, kiss me."

And he did. Bending his head, he tasted her, flicking his tongue over the fullness of her bottom lip. Taking in her taste, letting it seep into his being. He felt her arms go around his neck, and she arched to him for deeper contact.

He felt her nipples brush his chest and her hips come against his, and he plunged his tongue into her mouth, needing the invasion of her and hoping it didn't scare the hell out of her. But she didn't pull back. She opened her mouth even wider and pressed closer to him, moaning softly in her throat.

Lyndsey felt almost wanton, crazed in her need for this man. She welcomed his invasion, tasting him, loving it, and she pressed against him. Then as his mouth left hers and trailed fire along her skin, down her throat, she fell back in the bed, arching her body, waiting for the exquisite sensations she knew were coming.

Then his lips were at the pulse that beat wildly at her throat, and her nipples pulled painfully, the sensation running down to her belly and deep in her being. An ache began to build, a tightness that grew as R.J. swept his lips over her skin, found her nipple and took it in his mouth.

The pleasure she'd found earlier in the touch was pale compared to this sensation. She felt as if she was shattering, but in a most pleasant way, as if she was confetti being thrown into the air, full of color and sparkle, and going higher and higher on the wind. And every atom in her body was alive and filled with beauty.

She arched more, trying to get closer to the feeling, but knowing that this was just the fringe of what she could feel with R.J. She was free. She was soaring, and she felt wanted and desired.

R.J. brushed his fingers over her skin, then moved his hand lower. But as he touched the fastener at the waist of her jeans, he drew back from her breast. His breathing was ragged, his eyes dark with passion. "Is it all right?" he asked, and his asking for permission brought sharp tears to her eyes.

She touched his face, her fingers unsteady on the soft stubble of a beginning beard at his jaw, and she found she couldn't even speak a simple word like yes. It was so right, she didn't know how to tell him, so she showed him. She lowered her hand, covering his, then awkwardly tugged at the fastener until it popped open.

Chapter 13

Without taking her gaze away from R.J.'s, Lyndsey pulled the zipper down, then lifted her hips and slid the pants off. She kicked at them, shaking her feet free of them, then did the same with her panties. But R.J. helped, slipping them down her legs, then tossing them to the foot of the bed.

She lay very still, suddenly aware of not only being totally exposed to this man physically, but being totally exposed emotionally. She wanted and needed him. And she knew that the loving was only one-sided. But she wasn't going to stop this time. She wasn't going to deny herself this moment of being together. It would probably be all she had. And she knew that walking away from R.J. Tyler would be the most difficult thing she'd ever have to do.

She didn't want to think about that now, no more than she wanted to think about Rob, or the killer. She just wanted to get lost in the feelings and the loving. When

R.J. touched her stomach, then slid his hand down and curved it to her hip, she forgot everything but the moment. She turned to him, facing him on her side, her breasts aching for attention, and the center of her being throbbing and moist with desire.

His fingers flicked over her skin, down to her belly, then lower, and she froze for just a split second. Then she plunged headlong into the feelings and was shocked when she pressed herself against his hand. His mouth found hers again, his tongue darting into the moistness there, and at the same time his hand was stroking her, sending shivers of delight. He aroused her as gently as a summer breeze, yet the fire he was building in her was burning away every bit of fear she had.

His tongue darted in and out of her mouth, the rhythm suggestive and seductive, until her hips began to imitate the same beat. Pressing against his hand, then pulling back, then going to him again. "Yes," he whispered against her lips. "That's it, Lyndsey, that's it. Enjoy it. Want it."

And she did want it. She wanted everything he had. Then she felt his hand leave her and find her hand, closing over it, then gently drawing it down to him. "Feel how much I want you," he said and as she touched him, she felt him take in a sharp breath and shudder.

The knowledge that she had done this to him gave her a joy she couldn't explain. She wanted to shout to the world that R. J. Tyler wanted her, that he was touching her and making love to her. She closed her hand over him, feeling the heat and strength in him, and she knew the past was gone. This was all that real.

"Love me, R.J., please love me," she breathed as she wrapped her arms around his neck and tried to pull him over her.

Then he shifted and was on top of her, and she parted her legs willingly and held her breath when she felt him against her, testing her. Then there was a slow, gradual filling of the aching emptiness in her, and all of the loneliness she'd felt seemed to dissolve with the joining. She cried out from the happiness she felt, and R.J. froze.

"Did I hurt you?"

"No, no," she murmured, and she lifted her hips, trying to draw him as far as she could inside her. She wanted to erase the line where her body stopped and his body started. She wanted a oneness with this man that would make her a part of him forever.

Then he began to move, so gently at first that she was barely aware of it, until she felt a concentrated pleasure that grew and grew. As she began to rock her hips in time with his thrusts, she knew for the first time what sex was all about. It was pleasuring and sharing and caring, and for her, it was loving, an absolute love that defied description.

She held his shoulders, lifting her hips to meet him, her softness against his strength, and the sensations deep inside grew at an astounding rate. She threw back her head and closed her eyes, and she gave herself over to the pulsing rhythm until she felt as if she was going to splinter and that she would cease to exist.

Then light shot through her, a clean, blinding light that fragmented in her soul and burst into complete ecstasy. She was totally unconnected to anything but the man inside, and when she heard R.J. cry out, she knew a release that left her without the ability to do anything but just feel.

The sensations were intense and complete, then gradually she began to feel things beyond the pleasure. And she knew R.J. hadn't left her body, and it gave her happiness. He had his arm around her and rolled gently onto his side, hip to hip, breast to chest. And they laid there for what seemed forever.

His hand lifted to her face, his fingers touching her swollen lips. "Now, that's making love," he murmured. Yes, that's exactly what it had been for her. And now that she knew what it was, she wondered how she would ever live without it again.

He shifted, leaving her for just a moment before he pulled her to his side and held her against him.

"Thank you," she breathed, closing her eyes as she settled in the hollow of his shoulder.

"You're very welcome," he whispered, and his arm tightened on her.

Caught like that to him and feeling safer than she'd felt in the "safe place," she let herself drift into a place of deep, dreamless sleep.

When Lyndsey woke, the room was silvered by the light of a full moon. She felt R.J. beside her, and the weight of his arm resting on her waist was heavy and reassuring. She turned carefully without disturbing him and looked at him, his features bathed in the moonlight. She ached physically from making love, the tingling in her body pleasant and welcome, and she ached deep inside, but it wasn't a pleasant sensation.

She finally knew what love was. She knew what it felt like to love completely, and she knew what it was like to really make love. But the timing was all out of sync. She raised herself on one elbow, looking down at R.J., literally hurting in her heart at the sight of him in sleep.

How she fought the urge to touch him, to trace the line of his jaw with the tip of her finger, or trace the fullness of his bottom lip. How she wanted to renew his taste in her mouth, the feeling of his body over hers and filling hers.

But she couldn't. She turned to him, carefully easing his arm off her, then she slipped out of bed. He stirred for a moment, then settled with a sigh on his side. She loved him. He cared about her. She didn't doubt that, but that wasn't what she wanted. She wanted a complete love, a love of two people who couldn't live without each other, a love where it was one plus one making one whole person.

R.J. had had that before. He'd had it, and he didn't need it with her. It wasn't there, and she knew she couldn't settle for any less. She'd settled for less before, and she couldn't go through that again.

She suddenly needed fresh air, air that didn't seem saturated with the scent of R.J. and their lovemaking. Silently, she moved around the room, dressing quickly in jeans and a blue sweater, then she slipped on her running shoes. She hesitated for just a moment by the side of the bed, looking down at R.J., at his face washed in light and shadow from the glow of the moon. Each feature, each plane and angle was etched in her heart, and she would take the images with her. Memories for a tomorrow when there would be no R.J. in her life.

Then she turned quickly from the sight and hurried downstairs. She went to the door, opened it, and stepped out into the coolness of the evening. She stopped on the porch and looked out at the huge trees fringing the grass area that was illuminated by moonlight. The dark velvet of the sky was stark against the huge circle of the moon as it hung in the heavens.

Lyndsey inhaled, feeling her insides settle a bit, then she slowly went down the steps. She glanced at the garage with the lights on on the top floor. Then she moved across the grass toward the bluffs that overlooked the Sound.

She looked out at the water, dark and mysterious, and she could see Seattle to the west, and low glow of light fanning out into the night sky. The Olympic Peninsula was to the north, its rain forest a dark blur with a few flashing lights dotting the blackness.

She exhaled shakily and hugged herself tightly, as if she could literally hold herself together by that simple action. She loved R.J. It was that simple. It was something she never dreamed she would ever do in her life, love completely and fully. The first man she thought she loved wasn't capable of loving anyone, and the last man she'd loved wasn't capable of ever loving another person the way he had his wife. She'd really done it this time, and the old instinctive idea of running came back so strongly to her that she had to fight taking flight right then.

When this was over, when she knew what had happened and who was after her, then she'd disappear. It had worked once, running from physical pain, maybe it would work to run from this pain in her heart. She lifted her face to the sky, closing her eyes, but she opened them immediately when images of her time of loving with R.J. came to her full force. Her body tensed as her need for the man grew stronger than it had been before.

"Damn it," she muttered and turned to go back to the house, wondering how she would face the man again and act as if she could let go with some dignity, without falling apart completely.

As she turned, the shadow of a man came from nowhere, cutting between the lights from the house and where she stood on the bluffs. With his face in the darkness, he looked large and bulky, and the image was so much like Rob in silhouette that fear rose in her throat.

Then as she braced herself to run, he came closer, and even though she still couldn't make out his features, she could see the heavy jacket and the brilliant hunter's cap. The man she'd seen in the spyglass earlier, a policeman.

She let out a painfully tight breath. What had R.J. said his name was? Magee? That was it. Officer Dan Magee.

"You're Officer Magee aren't you?" she asked, straining to make out his features, but unable to.

He stopped several feet from her, hesitated, then nodded. "Yeah." His voice sounded rough and hoarse, as if he had a cold.

"Oh, you scared me," she breathed. "I forgot you two were out here. I know I should have stayed in the house, but it was so stuffy, and I needed fresh air. I'm just not used to a bodyguard."

As he came closer, not speaking, his hands in his pockets, she let out a held breath. "Can I stay outside for a while, just around here?" She wasn't ready to go back and face R.J. just yet. "I won't go any further."

He took another step toward her. "You shouldn't be out here," he said in a muffled rasp.

"I know, but I had to get out."

"Is the doc helping you?"

"Some, but it's so frustrating."

"How so?"

"I get to a certain point and it's blank."

He stood very still, then rasped, "Blank?"

"No face. I'm close, but it's still a blank."

He was silent for a long moment, then abruptly he motioned with one hand to the water behind her. "Do you want to walk by the water?"

She felt the cool night air brush her face and ruffle her hair. She held herself more tightly to control a faint trembling beginning in her. More distance between herself and R.J. was what she needed. "Could I?"

He glanced back at the house and the garage beyond it, then turned to Lyndsey. "If I go with you."

He abruptly turned and started back across the lawn area, motioning her to come with him. Quickly she went after him as he strode toward the far side of the house. "I thought we were going to the water?" she called as she hurried to catch up with him.

"We are," he said over his shoulder without turning back to her. "There's a path down this way."

She went after him, glancing once at the low light in the dormer windows of the house before turning from them and walking away with the man.

R.J. woke with a start, instantly out of a sleep that had been deep and restful. He knew immediately where he was and what had happened. And he knew immediately that Lyndsey wasn't beside him.

He lay very still, his eyes closed, remembering the past few hours. Trying to understand, yet knowing if he had forever, he could never understand the effect Lyndsey had on him. He'd wanted her since the beginning in one way or another, and lovemaking had been the culmination of what had seemed like a lifetime of that wanting instead of a few days.

He could feel the satisfaction still lingering in his body, yet at the same time he could feel the tugging of growing desire tightening the core of his being. He wanted her and wanted her and wanted her some more. And he knew that the wanting went well past just physical desire and was just as potent.

He opened his eyes, expecting to see the light on in the bathroom or Lyndsey moving around in the room somewhere, but she was nowhere to be seen. He listened, but there were no sounds from downstairs. Inhaling, he almost stopped breathing when he took in the scent of her that still clung to the bed linen and the very air that he breathed.

He was always a logical man. Maddy used to tease him about his need for logic; she'd laugh and say he couldn't find point "C" if he didn't go through "A" and "B" first. His breath caught in his chest, and he waited for the feeling that he'd betrayed her, that he'd broken the promises they'd made to each other.

But nothing like that came. There was a sense of completion to his time with Maddy, sadness that it was over, joy that he'd been with her, yet a sense of rightness about going on with life. He could barely take it in. After three years, he'd healed. It seemed like a miracle, then he knew that that miracle had come only after Lyndsey had entered into his life.

He rolled onto his side, then pushed himself up to sit on the edge of the bed. He buried his face in his hands, and in one stunning moment, he knew the real miracle. He loved Lyndsey. He loved her completely and wholly, and the idea scared the hell out of him. He'd done this once before, and it had been snatched away from him. He didn't know if he could survive losing that kind of love again.

He stood quickly and looked around, knowing that he had to see Lyndsey, he had to touch her and ground himself before he scattered into a million pieces. He grabbed his jeans and pushed his legs into them, then yanked up the zipper. Quickly he tugged a dark sweatshirt over his head and shoved his feet into sneakers.

Raking his fingers through his mussed hair, he headed downstairs.

If he could see Lyndsey, if he could look at her, he'd know if the idea of loving her was as frightening as it seemed in this room where he was all alone.

Lyndsey had to hurry to keep up with the policeman, taking several skipping steps as they went single file along a narrow path through heavy trees, then broke free into a clearing. But they weren't at the beach. They were still on the bluffs overlooking the Sound, but much farther from the house.

The man stopped about five feet ahead of Lyndscy and looked out over the water, silently gazing at the night all around them. "I thought we were going to the beach?" she said, thinking he'd taken the wrong path in the forest.

When he didn't answer her, she looked around, but instead of feeling soothed by nature, she felt more on edge than ever. She stared at the policeman, then went closer, moving nearer to the edge of the bluffs. She looked down at the beach at least forty feet below, even farther down than the bluffs by the house, then she looked up at the sky.

"Can we get to the beach?" she asked.

"Mmmm," he murmured.

She rubbed her upper arms with the flats of her hands, nervousness making her feel vaguely sick. "It's times like this that I wish I smoked so I'd have something to do with my hands," she said.

The man moved, taking something out of his pocket, then he turned and took a step toward her. "Gum," he said in his raspy voice. "That's how I quit smoking."

She looked at the foil that caught a glint of moonlight, then reached for it. Quickly she unwrapped the stick, and as she lifted it to her mouth, she stopped. She inhaled, and in a flash, she understood. Cloves. Clove gum. That night . . .

She lowered her hand without putting the gum in her mouth. "I remember."

"What?"

She saw herself, being grabbed, taking a sucking breath to scream and smelling cloves. "Strange. It's the gum. I smelled it. When he grabbed me, it was clove gum. I turned and . . ." She remembered. Turning. Being struck. Her glasses flying off from the blow to her face. Her glasses. She'd never seen who hit her. Just smelled clove gum in a world of blurring darks and lights. And she'd felt pain, smelled cloves and knew someone was trying to kill her.

"Oh, God, I have to get back. I have to tell R.J. so he can call Russ." She turned, but was abruptly stopped when the man grabbed her arm.

"Oh, no, you don't," he said, his voice low, but the roughness completely gone. And as he pulled her around to face him, he ground out, "You're not going to tell anyone anything, not ever."

R.J. hurried into the living room and stopped. He didn't see Lyndsey and he couldn't hear her. Worse yet, he could tell the house was completely empty. And strangely, he knew he would know if she was close by. He jogged through the house to the kitchen, flipped on a light and found the room empty. The bathroom door was open and the room dark. Then he crossed to the back door and tried it. It was locked.

He turned and went back through the house to the front door and stepped into the night. At the top step of the porch, he looked out into the silence of the shadows all around. Then he heard something, someone running from the garage coming toward the front of the house. The next instant Shields was running toward him.

"He's here! He got Magee. I found him by the garage. I've called for help, and Detective MacClain's office says he's on his way. He was taking the last ferry to come over."

R.J. knew instant and nauseating horror that he'd only felt once before in his life. He'd been right. If he loved Lyndsey, he was setting himself up for pain, yet in that instant he knew it was too late to even consider letting her out of his life. The pain would be worse without her.

"Keep the woman inside and lock the doors," Shields said as he unwrapped his gun from his shoulder holster.

"She's gone," R.J. said. "She's not in the house."

"Damn it," he muttered. "You get inside—"

"No, I'm going looking for her," R.J. said without giving it a second thought. "You go that way," he said, pointing to the driveway and garage area. "I'll go down to the water. Just give me a gun."

"This is all I've got," Shields said.

R.J. didn't wait for him to finish before he ran up the steps into the house. He found a flashlight in a box by the door, but nothing that could be used as an effective weapon. Then he saw the spyglass in the living room and remembered how Lyndsey had held it like a baseball bat trying to hit Mel. He picked it up and hurried back outside. Shields was already gone, and R.J. turned in the opposite direction. He took off at a run toward the trees to find the path down to the beach.

Each time his feet struck the ground, he felt a jolt go through his body, keeping time with a scattering of prayers that he was only vaguely aware of saying to himself. He couldn't lose Lyndsey. Not now. Not before he had even had a chance to love her the way she should be loved.

He broke into the trees and flipped on the flashlight. The weak beam hardly penetrated the thick darkness, but it was enough of a glow for R.J. to find the footpath. He ran along it, and he was going to swing to the right where the path to the water intersected the main route, when he thought he heard a sound. He stopped, looked to the west, down the trail that led to another lookout on the bluffs. He listened, but heard nothing except the night sounds.

Then a scream tore through the air, Lyndsey screaming "Help!"

Lyndsey stared up at the man who held her, and her eyes widened as he skimmed off the hunter's hat. At first she didn't understand, then she knew him. He wasn't at all like Rob, except for his size. He had dark eyes, with scraggly blond hair and flushed-looking skin. The man near the bank, the one who had bumped into her and knocked her glasses off.

"You," she whispered as stunning terror coursed through her.

"I knew you'd remembered me," he said. He had no idea she hadn't seen him that night. "But you'll never tell anyone," he said as he jerked her toward the edge of the bluffs.

She wasn't going to be his victim again. Never again. She lifted her free hand and swung at him, at the same time she screamed at the top of her lungs, "Help!"

Her hand struck his shoulder ineffectively, and before she could strike out again, he jerked her forward, then twisted her back against him, his other hand clamping like a vise over her mouth. In one motion, he had her off the ground, her feet flailing, making a sharp contact with his leg, yet he didn't seem to feel a thing.

"You're dead," he growled in her ear. "Dead. Just like the others. You'll all die."

She felt him spin around with her, making the world whirl sickeningly in front of her. But as she was being turned to the water, she caught a glimpse of something, a vision that she felt certain came from panic and lack of oxygen.

It looked like R.J. running out from the trees, and she wished it was true, that he was really here. Then she knew it was all true when she felt the killer jerk back in R.J.'s direction. His hold on her began to slip, and he took his hand away from her mouth. As soon as she sucked in air, she screamed at the top of her lungs. "It's him! It's him!"

The man uttered a violent curse, then literally threw her through the air. For an instant, she was certain she'd been pitched over the edge of the bluffs, but she felt her shoulder and hip painfully strike the hard ground. She rolled away further and scrambled to her feet. And as she turned, she saw R.J., and he wasn't a vision. He was real, and not more than ten feet from the killer. He was running full tilt at the man.

Then she saw the spyglass, saw R.J. lift it in the air and swing it in a full arc that only stopped when it struck the killer's head. As if in slow motion, the man staggered backward, teetered on the edge of the bluffs, then his arms spread at his side and he seemed to simply slip over the edge and out of sight.

There were no sounds, no scream, just a deadly silence.

She looked at R.J., saw him drop the spyglass on the ground, then she was running to him, into the shelter of his open arms, to be held tightly to his chest. She buried her face in the softness of his sweatshirt and felt his heart racing against her forehead. He had been as scared as she'd been. "He . . . he was going to . . ."

"Was that Rob?" he asked in a deep, ragged voice.

She closed her eyes tightly. "No, not Rob. He . . . he's from the bank, from outside. The man I told you bumped into me." Then she began to laugh, a strangled sound that hurt her chest. "And I never saw him when he attacked me. I never even saw him."

R.J. buried his fingers in her hair, cradling her head to him. "What do you mean?"

"My glasses. He hit me in the face and knocked my glasses off. He was just a blur, and all I really knew was he smelled of cloves and he was hurting me. That's why I thought he was Rob. The pain was everywhere."

Lyndsey trembled convulsively, and R.J. held her even tighter as he whispered, "You're safe. You're all right now." The words of the guide, but this was reality. Then reality deepened even more. "It's over, Lyndsey, it's finally over."

With those words, the hysterical laughter dissolved and she held on to R.J. so tightly her arms shook. "Yes, it's over," she echoed.

R.J. didn't move. He just held her and let her cry. And she knew, when the tears came, he thought she was crying from the shock. And maybe she was, partly, but she knew that the real tears were falling because he was right. It was over. What she had found with R.J. had come to an end.

At two o'clock in the morning there were lights on all over the property, and police cars, an ambulance and an investigative team swarmed over the crime scene. She could hear R.J. and Russ talking downstairs while she gathered her things together upstairs. She'd been surprised by Russ. After he'd been so intense and driven about the case, she'd expected him to be euphoric to have it over with. But he'd seemed almost let down, and he'd spoken to her in a flat tone of voice.

He'd found Rob, and that was why he'd decided to come over on the last ferry run to the island. Russ was at the house when R.J. and she had made their way back from the bluffs. Rob was in Houston, and he'd been there for over a week. He'd checked himself into a hospital, and his doctor wouldn't give any details, but Russ suspected he'd had a breakdown of sorts.

Lyndsey wasn't surprised by what Russ said, but shocked at her reaction. She'd actually felt sorry for Rob and really wished that he could find help. Less than a week ago, she would have felt some sense of satisfaction, maybe a feeling of revenge along with hope that he'd suffer.

But she'd changed. God, she'd changed. She'd almost died twice, and only now did she understand what it was to really live and to really love.

She stood in the center of the bedroom, unable to look at the bed with its mussed linen and the blankets in a heap on the floor. Quickly she walked to the bathroom, turned on the shower and stripped off her clothes. She stepped under the hot stream of water and let it wash over her. What now? Could she go on with her life just as if there had been no R.J. in it? The answer was there before the question was fully formed. No, she couldn't. But she'd go on. She'd make a life for herself, but she knew she'd never forget R.J., or stop wondering how he was, or looking for him when she woke in the morning, or wishing he was there when she went to sleep at night.

She began to rub her skin with a cotton cloth, but was unable to wash off the memory of his touch, of his hands on her, of the pleasures he'd given her. Pleasures she had never dreamed existed until now. She stopped, letting the cloth fall from her fingers to drop to the floor. She didn't want to lose that memory. That was all she'd have after tonight.

R.J. watched Russ talk to the coroner at the front door, then he came back into the living room. "Who'd ever have thought this place would be where this would all end?" he murmured as he went to the couch and dropped heavily onto the leather. He reached for his coffee and sat back, cradling the mug in his hands.

R.J. sat in the chair facing him and shifted low in it, resting his hands on the arms. "Lyndsey didn't even really meet the guy. Why would he fixate on her?"

Russ sipped some coffee, then looked at R.J. "That's the way it is with obsessive types. He saw her. She fit his image of women he thought should die, and he went after her. If she hadn't been at the bank on Fridays, he'd never have known she existed."

And if R.J. hadn't let Russ talk him into helping him, he never would have known she existed. The thought scared him. He couldn't begin to envision a world without Lyndsey in it. "Do you think that's the way he fingered all of his victims?"

"I can tell you that two of the women did business at that bank. That was one of the overlapping points of their lives. About the only one."

"God, the world's crazy," R.J. murmured.

"Yeah, so was Lionel Whittier."

"That's his name?"

"That's the name in his pocket. Probably that's as close as we'll get." Russ sipped more coffee, then asked. "What are you going to do now?"

R.J. shifted lower until his head rested on the chair back. "I think I'll get back into private practice. I didn't know how much I missed the one-on-one until—" He shrugged. "It's time."

"Yes, I'd say it's long past time, R.J." Russ stood and put his coffee on the side table. "I've got some work outside, then I'm heading back. Are you coming?"

"I am," R.J. heard Lyndsey say, then he looked up and saw her at the foot of the stairs, her tote in her hands.

Chapter 14

R.J. stood when she spoke, noticing the paleness of her skin and the way her hair clung damply at her temples. "You're leaving?"

"It's over. I need to get back." She looked at Russ. "Can I go back with you?"

"Sure, no problem."

R.J. knew she was walking out, and if she did, she'd never be back. He couldn't let her do that. He had to try to convince her that life was worth taking a chance. Heaven knew, he was taking the biggest chance he'd ever taken in his life by loving her.

She looked at R.J., her deep blue eyes stunning when they met his gaze. "I want to thank you for everything."

Polite words that seemed to come from a stranger. He'd only known her for a few days, but she was no stranger. She was as much a part of him as his own soul. "I need to talk to you before you go, Lyndsey."

She hesitated, her tongue darting out to touch her pale lips. "I could call you after I get home and settled."

"No. There're things I need to say here and now."

Her eyes widened, but she didn't refuse. Instead, she nodded, but didn't move into the room. "All right. As long as there's time before I leave."

Russ moved past her. "You've got time. I have to take care of something outside. I'll let you know when we're ready to take off."

"Thanks," she said softly, then put her tote down at the foot of the stairs.

R.J. felt as nervous as a teenager working up nerve to ask a girl out on his first date. But this was more than a date. This was his life. He motioned her into the room. "Sit down. It's been a long day."

She didn't move for a minute, then walked into the room and sat down on the far end of the couch, as far away from R.J. as she could get and still be in the room. "What did you want to talk about?" she asked.

He looked at her from where he stood, needing to touch her, to hold her, yet knowing he couldn't. Not yet. "Us," he said simply.

"There is no 'us'," she said without hesitating.

He tightened inside. "That sounds like a line from a very bad movie."

"This isn't a movie," she said, her eyes staring at her hands clasped on her lap. "No guaranteed happy endings, just an ending."

He couldn't stand the distance anymore. He went to her, but didn't touch her. Instead, he dropped to his haunches in front of her and waited until she looked up into his eyes. "Lyndsey, you're right. There are no guaranteed happy endings in this life. There are no guarantees, except a guarantee that there are no guarantees. Life's moment to moment.''

He watched her hands tighten in her lap until her knuckles were bloodless. "I know," she whispered, "I know."

"No, you don't. All you know is what you've gone through before. What Rob did to you. But that's not what you can have." He reached out then, covering her hands with his. "I love you. I never thought I'd say that again in this life, but I really love you."

He didn't know what reaction he expected, but it wasn't her jerking away from him and getting awkwardly to her feet to push past him. It wasn't her silently moving toward the door and stooping to pick up her bag.

"Didn't you hear me?" he asked. "I said I love you."

She stopped and spoke without turning. "No, you don't."

"What do you mean, I don't?"

"You love the idea of love. You loved your wife and you want that again."

"Damn straight I do," he said honestly, staying where he was by the couch.

She turned then, and he could see the brightness of tears in her eyes. "And I can't give it to you, R.J. I can't be her. I can't help you get that back. I wish I could, I really do, but I can't."

He saw her take an unsteady breath, and that's when he moved. He went to her, but he stopped two feet in front of her and didn't touch her. "Is that what you think this is all about? That I want you to take Maddy's place?"

She dropped her bag at her feet with a thud, and hugged herself with her arms. "I know what you had with her. I know that you'll never love anyone like that again."

"No, I won't. I couldn't," he said softly.

Lyndsey looked at R.J., her heart breaking more and more with each word he uttered. She knew it. She'd known it all along, and yet she'd let herself fall in love with him. "I know," she whispered and hoped she wouldn't cry in front of him.

"What do you think my life was with Maddy?"

She stared at him, unable to even think of that time in his life without pain radiating through her. "I...I don't know."

"I'll tell you what it was like. We loved and we laughed and we were there for each other. We never had children. She couldn't, and it broke her heart. And we talked about adopting, then we put it off until we knew our lives were set in patterns that we didn't want to alter."

She didn't want to hear all this. And she had to fight the need to put her hands over her ears.

"We loved each other. I loved her completely. She was my life."

"Stop," she managed in a tight voice.

But he didn't. "And I found out that loving a person doesn't stop when they die. I had wished it had a lot of times, I prayed it would, but now I'm glad it didn't."

"R.J., you don't have to say this."

"Oh, yes I do. I need you to understand that when I love, I love completely. I don't love because it's fashionable, or because it's convenient, or because I need someone in my bed, or even because I'm lonely. When I love, it's because of the person I'm with."

"That's all it is. I'm here. I'm with you."

"And it was convenient for me to fall in love and take you to bed, is that it?"

She felt heat burn her face, but she nodded. "Yes, I mean, no, I . . ."

"You mean yes. You have no idea how much someone could love you simply because of who you are and what you are, do you?"

"I . . . I . . ."

"Let me set things straight. I love you because I saw you in that bed bruised and cut and holding on to life. I love you because you trusted me, and you let me be with you. And I love you because you're who you are. You aren't Maddy. No one is. But no one's Lyndsey, either."

"You don't—"

"Answer me one question?" he cut in.

She nodded, unable to say even a simple word.

"Do you love me?"

She held herself more tightly, trying to stop the shaking that she felt in her soul. "That's not fair."

"Just answer me, Lyndsey. You owe me that much before you leave me."

She stared at him, at the image of the man she knew she was going to carry in her soul for the rest of her life. "Yes, but—"

"No buts. Let me make this simple for both of us. I don't love you because I'm lonely, and I don't love you because I'm looking for a substitute for what I had. I love you because you're Lyndsey and I can't live without you. I've heard that love is lovelier the second time around. I don't know about that, but I know that I've been given a chance at real love for a second time. A love that I can't walk away from."

She stared at him, daring to let his words into her heart, feeling as if she could barely breathe.

"I'm older than you, and I've lived longer. I show some wear, some gray hair, but I'm loyal and I'm damn sure that you're the one person in this world that I want to spend the rest of my life with, whether that's ten minutes or fifty years." His face broke into a gentle smile that lit her world with the most wonderful glow. "Although if I have any say in it, I'm rooting for the fifty years."

The door opened right then, and Russ looked inside. "Are you about ready to go, Lyndsey?" he called.

R.J. took another step toward her and didn't look away when he spoke. "Well, Lyndsey, are you ready to leave?"

She stared at him, into the depths of his eyes, and she felt everything slip into place. "No, I'm not ready," she said without taking her eyes off R.J.

"How much longer are you going to be?" Russ called.

She let the smile in her soul touch her lips, and she took a step toward R.J. Hesitantly she reached out, spreading her hands on his chest, loving the feel of his heart beating against her palms.

"Lyndsey, how much longer?" Russ called again.

"About fifty years," she whispered to R.J.

"What?" Russ asked.

R.J. looked over her head at Russ. "She's staying here," he said and pulled her to him. "She's staying with me."

Lyndsey didn't hear what Russ said, but she did hear the door shut and, a moment later, a car drive off. Then she tipped her head back and looked up at R.J. "Are you sure?"

"Are *you* sure?" he echoed.

She touched his face, letting her fingers rest on his jaw where a pulse was beating wildly. He was as scared by all this as she was. "Yes, I am," she whispered. "I've never been more sure of anything in my life."

R.J. smiled, then lowered his head, and his lips found hers. Lyndsey had come to Seattle to make a new life for herself, but she'd never expected to find the missing part of her soul, the part that made her whole for the first time in her life.

Lyndsey watched R.J. come back into the bedroom, the cool light of dawn etching his face in planes and shadows. He'd been with her all night, long after the last car had left and the ambulance had gone. And the love she felt for him only grew each passing moment they were together.

"That was Russ on the phone," he said as he stopped at the end of the bed, his face set in grim lines as he gripped the footboard with both hands. He leaned forward as he spoke. "He says one of the men at the hospital recognized Whittier as a maintenance man he saw there on your floor. The hospital has no record of him working there. They figure he stole a uniform, started the fire to get into your room, and found out where you were by calling my office."

"What?"

"Russ found out a doctor called my office to get in touch with me. I've done a lot of consultation work with this particular doctor, and my assistant got to talking to him and told him I was fishing up here."

She was beginning to tremble inside being reminded of what had happened. Amazingly enough, she'd almost forgotten about it until now. "What does the doctor have to do with this?"

"Nothing at all. He's been in Europe for a month."

"He . . . Whittier pretended he was the doctor?"

"Probably. He was totally obsessed with finishing what he'd started with you."

"If he had stayed away, I wouldn't have been able to implicate him. I never really saw him," she breathed.

"But he didn't know that, and he couldn't stay away," R.J. said, then stood straight and ran both hands roughly over his face. "And we'll never understand that, no more than we'll understand why he wanted to kill blond, blue-eyed women. But it makes good copy." He grimaced. "Speaking of which, Russ says that a gang of reporters is camped at the ferry dock. He wanted us to be prepared."

She watched him unzip his pants, then as he casually stripped the denim off his body, she felt her breath catch at the sight of him naked. Would she ever get used to the sight of him, of that instant wanting and need that filled? She hoped not. No, she knew she wouldn't.

Then she caught on his last words, and she sat up, not bothering with the sheet to cover her own nakedness. Any modesty or embarrassment had been banished during the night. "Reporters?"

"The papers got hold of the story as soon as the call went in." He came to the bed, his bare feet silent on the hardwood floor. "It can't be helped."

She shook her head. "I never thought of that. If they get my name and background, Rob can find me." She started to get out of bed. "I can't let that happen."

"Hey, hold on," R.J. said as he came to her, touching her on the shoulders so she couldn't get up. Then he slipped into bed with her, easing her back down, and supporting himself on one elbow as he lightly cupped her chin with the other hand. He was inches from her face, looking into her eyes. "No more running, love. I won't let anything happen to you. Trust me."

She scanned his face, her gaze flicking from the intensity in his eyes to the darkening of a new beard on his jaw, to the set line of his mouth. "But, Rob—"

His hold tightened on her. "Do you love me?"

She looked him right in the eye. "You know I do."

"Do you trust me and believe that I'd never lie to you?"

She touched her tongue to her lips. She did trust him, in every way, completely, or she couldn't have given herself to him the way she had. And that was so new to her, she didn't really understand it. She didn't know if she ever would, but she accepted it as part of her new life. "I do."

"I like those words," he murmured, a gentle smile curling his lips. "Remember them and say them again in three days."

"Three days?"

"Just long enough for blood tests and getting the license." He bent over her to brush his lips across hers, then he drew back. "Will you marry me, Lyndsey?"

Lyndsey didn't hesitate. "Yes." She reached out to R.J., wrapping her arms around him and pressing her lips to the hollow of his throat.

"Good, now that's settled, we've got about an hour before we have to leave to catch the ferry." His hand ran lightly over the line of her bare hip, brushing a trail of fire, and she felt her breasts swelling.

No, she would never get enough of this man. She tasted his skin, feeling the heat of his heart against her lips and his touch resting on her thigh. Then they were together, body against body, their heat mingling to start a fire.

His hands explored her, feathering over the swelling of her hips, then trailed to her stomach. But instead of going lower to the throbbing that grew with each passing heartbeat, his hand went higher to her breasts and cupped the swollen fullness gently. Her nipples peaked, and she took a gasping breath.

"An hour?" she asked in a unsteady breath.

"For now. Later we'll have a lifetime," he whispered, his breath sweet on her skin.

That brought tears to her eyes, and she felt so happy she could barely take it in. "Yes, a lifetime," she echoed.

"R.J.," he said as he nibbled at her ear.

"Wh...what?"

He drew back and looked down into her face with eyes alive with the same hunger she knew was echoed in hers. "My name, it's R.J."

She didn't understand. She touched his lips with her fingertips. "I know that."

"No, you don't. That's it. It's R.J., period."

"The initials?"

"That's it. That's all there is. I thought you should know since we're getting married and you're the closest person to me in this world."

"Just the initials?" she asked, a smile coming with such ease that she felt pleasure from the simple ability to let it happen. "Nothing more?" she teased. "No Reginald, or Rothschild?"

"No." He shook his head. "My grandfather was R. Tyler. My father was J. Tyler. And I'm just R.J. An old southern tradition."

She laughed and felt a tingle go through her whole body. "You could never be *just* R.J.," she said softly, her voice catching on the words as the intensity of her love for the man grew by leaps and bounds. "Never."

He brushed her full bottom lip with the ball of his thumb. "If you ever decide you want children—"

"When," she corrected him, "not if."

His touch on her stilled, and his eyes narrowed. "Do you mean that, after everything that happened before?"

"Yes, I do, maybe because of what happened before," she said as she pushed the memories into the past, memories that felt as if they belonged to another life. "I want *your* child."

"God, I love you," he said and gave her a hard, fierce kiss, then pulled back, his breathing more ragged and uneven with each passing moment. "All right, but promise me one thing, that they'll have full names."

"You don't want to call them 'A' or 'B' or 'C'?"

He laughed, a wonderful sound that skimmed over her nerves and settled into the core of her soul. "Heavens, no. Maybe Lyndsey with a middle name, but no letters."

"No letters," she agreed as she took his hand and drew it down to her heart. "Maybe Rutherford or Rothschild, or Richy Joe," she said, her laughter smothered as R.J. covered her mouth with his.

"We'll discuss this later," he said against her lips.

"In an hour," she agreed, and knew without a doubt that the new life she'd vowed to start when she had flown out of Dallas had just begun.

* * * * *

This is the season of giving, and Silhouette proudly offers you its sixth annual Christmas collection.

SILHOUETTE

Christmas Stories

1991

Experience the joys of a holiday romance and treasure these heartwarming stories by four award-winning Silhouette authors:

Phyllis Halldorson—"A Memorable Noel"
Peggy Webb—"I Heard the Rabbits Singing"
Naomi Horton—"Dreaming of Angels"
Heather Graham Pozzessere—"The Christmas Bride"

Discover this yuletide celebration—sit back and enjoy Silhouette's Christmas gift of love.

YOU'VE ASKED FOR IT, YOU'VE GOT IT!

MAN OF THE MONTH: 1992

ONLY FROM
🕊 SILHOUETTE® *Desire*™

You just couldn't get enough of them, those sexy men from Silhouette Desire—twelve sinfully sexy, delightfully devilish heroes. Some will make you sweat, some will make you sigh . . . but every long, lean one of them will have you swooning. So here they are, men we couldn't resist bringing to you for one more year. . . .

A KNIGHT IN TARNISHED ARMOR
by Ann Major in January

THE BLACK SHEEP
by Laura Leone in February

THE CASE OF THE MESMERIZING BOSS
by Diana Palmer in March

DREAM MENDER
by Sheryl Woods in April

WHERE THERE IS LOVE
by Annette Broadrick in May

BEST MAN FOR THE JOB
by Dixie Browning in June

Don't let these men get away! *Man of the Month*, only in Silhouette Desire.

Angels Everywhere!

Everything's turning up angels at Silhouette. In November, Ann Williams's ANGEL ON MY SHOULDER (IM #408, $3.29) features a heroine who's absolutely heavenly—and we mean that literally! Her name is Cassandra, and once she comes down to earth, her whole picture of life—and love—undergoes a pretty radical change.

Then, in December, it's time for ANGEL FOR HIRE (D #680, $2.79) from Justine Davis. This time it's hero Michael Justice who brings a touch of out-of-this-world magic to the story. Talk about a match made in heaven . . . !

Look for both these spectacular stories wherever you buy books. But look soon—because they're going to be flying off the shelves as if they had wings!

Silhouette Special Edition

is pleased to announce

WEDDING DUET
by Patricia McLinn

Wedding fever! There are times when marriage must be catching. One couple decides to tie the knot, and suddenly everyone they know seems headed down the aisle. Patricia McLinn's WEDDING DUET lets you share the excitement of such a time.

December: PRELUDE TO A WEDDING (SE #712) Bette Wharton knew what she wanted—marriage, a home . . . and Paul Monroe. But was there any chance that a fun-loving free spirit like Paul would share her dreams of meeting at the altar?

January: WEDDING PARTY (SE #718) Paul and Bette's wedding was a terrific chance to renew old friendships. But walking down the aisle had bridesmaid Tris Donlin and best man Michael Dickinson rethinking what friendship really meant. . . .

Take 4 bestselling love stories FREE

Plus get a FREE surprise gift!

NORA ROBERTS

Love has a language all its own, and for centuries, flowers have symbolized love's finest expression. Discover the language of flowers—and love—in this romantic collection of 48 favorite books by bestselling author Nora Roberts.

Starting in February 1992, two titles will be available each month at your favorite retail outlet.

In February, look for:

Irish Thoroughbred, Volume #1
The Law Is A Lady, Volume #2

Collect all 48 titles and become fluent in the Language of Love.

LOL192

THE LANGUAGE of LOVE